KIDDAR'S LUCK

PHOTOGRAPH OF HOLDER

Signature of Holder

C96488

JACK COMMON

Kiddar's Luck

BLOODAXE BOOKS

ISBN: 978 1 85224 127 8

This edition published 1990 by
Bloodaxe Books Ltd,
Eastburn,
South Park,
Hexham,
Northumberland NE46 1BS.

Original edition first published 1951 by
the Turnstile Press, London.
Second edition published 1975 by
Frank Graham, Newcastle upon Tyne.

www.bloodaxebooks.com
For further information about Bloodaxe titles
please visit our website or write to
the above address for a catalogue.

Supported by
**ARTS COUNCIL
ENGLAND**

Digital reprint of the 1990 Bloodaxe Books edition.

ACKNOWLEDGEMENTS

The front cover photograph shows Heaton Road, Newcastle, in 1905, reproduced by kind permission of Newcastle City Libraries & Arts. The smaller photographs of Jack Common – aged 3 and 17 – are from the Jack Common Archive at the University of Newcastle upon Tyne, reproduced by kind permission of Jack Common's daughter, Mrs Sally Magill.

Acknowledgements and thanks are due to the following people for their help: Mrs Sally Magill; Frank Graham; Christine Moyes of Blackie and Son Ltd; Lesley Gordon, Special Collections Librarian at the University of Newcastle upon Tyne; Eileen Aird, compiler of the Jack Common Archive; and Frank Manders of Newcastle City Libraries.

Hallo, kidders! How's yor luck?—JIMMY LEARMOUTH
(*At the Newcastle Hippodrome*)

KIDDAR'S LUCK

Chapter One

BLUNDER BY AN UNBORN BABE

She was a fool, of course, my mother. Her mother said so: 'Bella is a fool, I'm afraid, a weak fool. Here she is marrying a common workman, one who drinks and is not a good Christian. She will never know happiness now.' You would think the old lady was great shakes herself to hear her. And she was in her way. Not that she had any money ever, but she made poverty respectable. She brought up a large family in a small upstairs flat in Bath Lane Terrace under the hazard of a husband frequently sacked from a large number and variety of jobs for drinking. At her back-door lay the middens of the Oystershell Lane slum but the front looked out on a row of freshly-whitened doorsteps and well-polished door-handles. The family attitude had to be eyes front, while she kept the back-door slum at bay with a Bible, a black cape and a trick of grinding her teeth at anyone who crossed her. She reigned there like another Queen Victoria, orbed and sceptred against the threat of commonness and firm in her knowledge that if ever poverty got the better of respectability she'd see her family sink into the nineteenth-century maelstrom of casual labour, drinking, pawning, wife-beating and gaol.

My father respected her, but could never come under her command. He stood over her like a northern barbarian, too huge for her reprimand, making jokes about Jesus, and every now and then rising on his toes and bringing his whole weight back on his heels so that the old house shook, and the flower-vase standing on the family Bible trembled and looked like toppling over. He won, but was doomed. The old lady and the Old Testament knew. They were right.

True, my parents made a handsome couple but, though they did not know this then were totally unsuited to one another. They were brought into each other's orbit purely by chance. It happened in the street. My mother had a regular date with two girl-friends going to the theatre, sitting in the gallery where they ate chocolates, were more or less enraptured with the show and delighted to be just girls together. I expect that was wearing thin a bit, though, as the moving years began to point to thirty. Anyway, they came out into the gas-lit street one night, linking arms so as to make a way along the crowded

1

pavements and not get swept under the passing horse-trams which were the main traffic menace of the period. Three shop-girls, all bright and happy, one blonde with puffed-out frizzy hair; one pleasant-faced, but marred by a large birthmark down her cheek; and my mother, dark-ringleted and ruddy as a rose, with delicately-tiny curled nostrils and peeping black eyes, all laughing and talking as they swayed in and out the mixed Saturday night crowd. The main-street pubs they passed flared with rows of gas-jets, their brass doors flashing as they swung. From one of them a group of young men stag-gered out, flushed and noisy with drink. The girls were halted temporarily to a barrage of street-cracks—'Oh, oh, what-ho, she bumps! Does your mother know you're out? My, ain't she lovely!' and so on. The last of the young men to come out of the pub stood over the rest, handsome and gigantic. As the girls giggled and looked down at each other edging away, this man pushed through the others making towards my mother. Whatever he was going to say he didn't. But my mother had seen something in his face and when they were free of the group she alone turned her head. He stood there still, his pals trying to move him on. Seeing her look, he suddenly pointed and loudly called, 'That girl, the one with the curls, that's the girl I'm going to marry.'

He did too. The marriage took place precisely as announced outside the Westgate Road boozer that Saturday night, and *he was drunk on his wedding day*. The doom was working out already, you see. Both ways, for mother was quite unreason-ably upset over an occurrence which seemed quite normal in his circle, so loggerheads were appearing right from the start. She soon learned what the old lady had in mind when she deplored marriage to a working-man. The old lady was no snob, she believed in work and was harsh on idlers even if they had money, but she knew what a working-man's wife had to put up with. My father was now a locomotive fire-man, earning about eighteen shillings a week in hours that varied from fourteen to sixteen a day, all round the clock. Compared to this his wife had a lady's life, earning more than he did as cashier in a wholesale jeweller's with a bit of buy-ing and selling on the side. Her leisure was full, too. She sang in a choir, she danced (at highly respectable balls), she read a great deal, she went to church and to theatres. He had hardly time to live.

His job dictated even where they must live. It had to be in the calling area close to the engine sheds, so that the caller (or knocker-up) could reach him any hour of the night. There'd be a sharp rapping of heels along the pavement, a quick knock, father's yawning 'Hallow', and the caller's cry

2

'Three-twenty-five, Special to York. D'ye hear?' 'Aye, aye, three-twenty-five', my father groaned and so did the bed as he heaved out. At first, mother wanted to get up and make him breakfast, but he wouldn't have that. 'Had away back to bed, woman, I'll do for meself.' She was allowed to put up his bait and that was all. So she lay listening to him putting on the kettle, splashing through his wash, giving vent to a loud fart now and then, and finally banging his way out to the quiet street without any good-byes. He wanted no fuss about the dull matter of going to work.

But the long hours he was away hung drearily on her. She was ambitious of making money by the mysterious process of 'buying and selling', and to that end attended auction sales, bought bargains and advertised them for sale again in the local paper. Her triumphs were nothing to father, though; he thought the whole thing dishonest, and a reflection on his own inability to earn much money. Moreover, he didn't like her gadding about and he had the general fear of the railwaymen of that period that their absences would be taken advantage of and adultery go on behind their backs. In any case, more often than not it was an empty house she returned to, an empty house in a hateful suburb. She loved the town and was happiest in company, with the full household of her childhood. True, she was very much in love with her husband. She'd sit up far into the night waiting for his return, a pleasant enough parcel of pretty wifehood for any man to find at the end of the day's work. But he didn't like it. He was shamed, shamed in his manhood that he was kept like a slave away from her and could only slink back in the late hours when work had done with him and left him too tired and irritable to toss the nice nothings of love towards his waiting fancy. He spoke sharp and hurt her. He didn't want to hear about the people she'd met in town that day; if they were men, they were possible rivals that might take advantage of her loneliness; if they were women they would tend to take her back to her own world. She didn't know that he felt this. She knew that he admired her, but not that he resented his cultural inferiority to her. During their courtship,. for instance, he painfully taught himself to write because she wanted letters from him when a backshift submerged him for a week, sitting shirt-sleeved in his lodgings and slowly pushing a fist round the curves of some conventional phrase —only to be told later that there was nothing in his letters. When she wanted to show off her handsome husband-to-be to her friends, the occasion was always spoilt. The women fell for him, of course, and weren't very kind to her in consequence. The men tended to talk very cleverly on topics they

3

felt sure he was ignorant of; then when he came into the conversation it was with the loud voice of a man used to talking above the noise of a running locomotive* and a ruthlessness of debate which they thought caddish. He was shy, of course. He didn't look it, and she never suspected it, but he was shy. Not knowing what was biting him, so to speak, she was disappointed to be brusquely ordered off to bed with all her little tales untold and her niceness going for nothing.

Then the baby came, a lovely babe—not me, I don't mean. A golden little girl, pretty as a picture, with a smiling temperament that kept a warm content about her so that she lay cosy in her cot, never crying and no trouble at all. She died. Meningitis at eleven months. Mother was too ill to go to the funeral. When she got up, the house was intolerably empty and she kept coming across baby's things, a sock or a little bonnet, to madden her grief. Some neighbours told her to go to the grave. She didn't know where it was, but she took flowers, rain-washed chrysanthemums tangy with their winter scent, and walked the long pathways of the cemetery against dark gusts and the swish of flung rain, straight to the spot. A small heap of yellow clay, that was it, not far from the wall or from a hawthorn black and broken in its winter weathering. She knelt down and the flowers fell from her hands, bedraggled heads of weak pink and rust and a yellow tawdry against the other yellow of the clay. She must have stayed there a long time, but in telling this story she never got beyond that point, so that what agony she had, or what release, I never knew. She never again bought chrysanthemums....

Now there was an already stricken field, which future infants would do well to avoid you'd think. That I didn't is my curious chronicle. No doubt the correct thing is to begin it as you would any life-story with the birth of the hero. Doing so, you excite sympathy and wonder right away by exhibiting a tender puling scrap of humanity which every reader knows is soon to be dignified by the tremendous name of John Bigshot, or what it is; and that coming greatness hangs like a halo over the cradle. There's quite a kick in the contrast. Can't make it in my case, however. No greatness, you see, nothing to come; no magic name dangling over the infant Kiddar for him to grow towards. The fact is, before this particular birth, as before many that never get into story, a blunder was made. It was a bad one and it spoilt my autobiography in advance.

It happened at conception. Now how a child is conceived is still largely anybody's guess. For many centuries people thought it was just one of the things women did, a feminine mystery best not thought about, one of the troubles of an

4

always-troubled sex. Then for some more centuries, men held to the notion that *they* did it. With their seed. They saw that the soil when sown put out corn; and woman, too, if given the seed was another, warmer earth which brought forth babes. That belief held good till about 1828, by which time a certain amount of double-thinking had set in with the result that there was discovered an equivalent of the male seed in the female, the ovaries. This made conception a dual affair, like the act leading to it. So to be perfectly just to both parties, we began to assume that each little sperm from the male was loaded with a packet of genes, and each ovum in the female was similarly equipped. Consider genes as a sort of ancestral dust, progenitors' traits mummified and microfied into spores from a family tree, and you've got the idea. The two packets collide; there is a resultant tangle and sorting-out which ends by producing one of us, or one of them, as the case might be.

That may be a true account of what happened when I first began to occur but I doubt it. Doubt any theory, I feel, which is so wonderfully appropriate to the times, being altogether medical, chemical, physical, and having that gritty look which shows it to be sediment from minds so constantly engaged in reductive analysis that they are not likely to light up the *whole* of this ghostly Armageddon of the generations we call the act of conception. However, that's it, as we see it now, and it is the operation I was about to take part in one cold November night in the year 1902 when me and my genes were hanging about on the other side of Time, corporeally uncommitted and the whole world of Chance open to us. It was then we made a mess of things.

There were plenty of golden opportunities going that night. In palace and mansion flat, in hall and manor and new central-heated 'Cottage', the wealthy, talented and beautiful lay coupled—welcome wombs were ten-a-penny, must have been. What do you think I picked on, me and my genes, that is? Missing lush Sussex, the Surrey soft spots, affluent Mayfair and gold-filled Golder's Green, fat Norfolk rectories, the Dukeries, and many a solid Yorkshire village, to name only some obvious marks, I came upon the frost-rimed roofs of a working-class suburb in Newcastle-upon-Tyne, and in the back-bedroom of an upstairs flat in a street parallel with the railway line, on which a halted engine whistled to be let through the junction, I chose my future parents. There, it was done. By the time that engine took its rightaway and rolled into the blue glare of the junction arcs, another kiddar was started, an event, one might add, of no novelty in that quarter and momentous only to me.

I at once came under the minus-sign which society had

already placed upon my parents. They were of no account, not even overdrawn or marked 'R.D.', people who worked for a living and got just that, who had a home only so long as they paid the weekly rent, and who could provide for offspring by the simple method of doing without themselves. I had picked the bottom rung of the ladder with a vengeance, for it was that kind of ladder used in the imaginations of mathematicians, on which the rungs mount in minus degrees and the top is crowned with no opulence of over-plus but with the mere integer. A sad mistake; though millions make it I think it still deserves a mourning wreath.

Naturally, there were some bad fairies gathered round the bed at such a conception. One, somewhat like a tramp, chalked upon the bedstead the sign which means 'No hand-outs here'; another, four-belted as a ghostly navvy, swung his pick in promise of future hard work; a blear-eyed one, faintly lit up, lifted the bottle; and one looking like a magistrate made a bitter mouth over the syllables of an unspoken 'Borstal'. There was a good fairy, too—must be. Something fairly shapeless, I imagine, with no sign of concrete blessing but a kind of cheerful scintillation which had the look of coming glory only you couldn't guess what it was. That would be there certainly. Every child conceived is unique, utterly new, a wonder in its own right. You can count the sad probabilities of its likely fate as you count its toes—and the piggy gets none. Yet for a time there stays this chance of miracle: the new-comer *may* prove a golden lad or lass in whose Midas-soul multitudes of genes are re-minted, so that qualities muted or dormant in ordinary men with this one come ringing into currency. Well, then, there was a time when I had that possibility, as you had, as all have; it didn't last long and it wasn't much—the bastard's mite, you could call it. Owing to my fatal choice that, in fact, was all I could come into the world with.

Of course, I wasn't into the world yet. Nobody for a while was even aware of my existence. I must have been but I've forgotten all about it long ago. It is not remembering that lasts but remembering what one has remembered. A baby remembers having suckled yesterday and so knows how to suckle today but when it grows up it won't have any particular memory of suckling it can recall and refer to. The thing was physical, not reflective, and it is gone. I cannot remember my time in the womb, yet, though not a full citizen in any sense of the word, I was in being definitely and already affecting my parents' lives from the moment they became aware of my existence. For that matter, they were affecting me.

These dissonances and anxieties gathered about the family I'd landed in could not penetrate, perhaps, the coma of the

6

pre-natal period, but fear may have done so. My mother feared for me before I was born and I think some of that fear seeped into my unawakened soul and already stained the expectancy which the comer from eternity must have with a twinge of the first cramp and contraction of mortal time. I was a second bet in what might be a losing sequence, the favourite for the first race having gone down, and so when it was my turn to come under starter's orders, I certainly wasn't odds-on.

Fear is a bad bedmate any time, and particularly so in the bed of childbirth. Fear was very present in that back bedroom one hot August Saturday very early in the small hours, so-called. Small? In the sense that some beers were called 'small', yes, and that these hours are similarly weak and soon-sped for those asleep or half-asleep. Large, tedious hours they are if one is awake to experience them. My mother was awake. She lay feeling the slow early pains and trying to judge by the light what time it was. There was a clock in the bedroom, but it hung on the wall above the fireplace and next to the window, so that the glow from the summer sky dimmed its dial. She waited for the strike, unwilling to disturb her husband much before the caller did. The clock didn't strike, and she thought, as she would think, that it must be out of order. So she eased herself heavily out of the warm blankets which father insisted on having all the year round, and moved into the kitchen. Another clock stood there, and as the gas-mantle plopped to her lit match (she could never light the gas properly), its hands showed ten to two. Nearly an hour yet before the caller came, plenty of time.

She put a kettle on the gas-stove in the scullery and stood looking out into the faint August night. There was the back-yard below, long black clothes-props leaning against the corner walls; blind houses over the lane, their dim slate roofs stretching away as far as one could see to where a glow on the sky stood over the heart of the town. She leant with her knuckles on the scullery bench, her heavy body sagging to the recurrent pluck of pain. I must get him up, she was thinking, he must go for Mrs. Crocker, but I'll make his breakfast, put him in a good temper, bacon, there should be three rashers left—I hope it's not a girl, oh God, not a girl. . . .

My father, when roused, said it was all a fuss about nothing, and she was a fool and a faddy; there was plenty of time, and wasn't she just imagining it anyway. She wept, wanting sympathy, and that annoyed him enough to get him moving. He shoved her out of the way (there was never much room in that scullery), and was soon splashing under the tap, concluding with his usual violent blowing on his nose, and a slinging of

7

snot into the sink. 'You go back to bed,' he ordered, 'while I get the old geezer.' And he went.

He had that midwife there in double-quick time, too, the old dear mightily uncomfortable because her hair-pins weren't in properly and her hat kept sliding. She looked a sight, she felt, and wasn't helped to confidence by my father's scorn for anybody who wasn't instantly ready for a job they'd promised to do. However, the caller had been during his absence; he sat down to his bacon, and ate rapidly—it was a sure thing he wouldn't be late for his job.

Some fifteen hours later he returned, complete with a bottle of whisky to wet the baby's head with. But—no baby. Neighbours had been in and out all day, with various words of sympathy and advice, and citations of parallel cases mostly of a gloomy character. They fled when he appeared. Mother wanted a doctor, so did midwife (especially now that *he* was back). Father said, 'I didn't think *you'd* be any good on the job,' and went to fetch expert aid.

For the next two hours, he and the doctor sat drinking whisky and arguing about British imperialism as evidenced in the late Boer War—my father was pro-Boer, at least he was against anybody who wasn't—while I and my mother fought to get me born. I don't remember it. But from hearsay and later knowledge, it is easy to reconstruct the setting, so very like a problem picture of the period. A large brass bedstead took up most of the little room, a marble-topped wash-stand, a chest of drawers, ochre-tinted lace curtains at the window, and many pictures in large frames breaking up the rose-and-two-leaf pattern on a cream wallpaper. There was a very weak gaslight washing over the scene in which the doctor was now in charge, very impressive he was too, with his high forehead, long silken beard and the gold cuff-links on his rolled sleeves. Mrs. Crocker, the good soul, stood rocking from one foot to the other in anxiety; and my mother's usual high colour flushed now under a wet-chalk brow and curls damp and diminished as a result of her long anguish. Father next door was two whiskies up on the doctor when with his aid and mother's latest agony, I put my little barque of life into this world of time and crumbling days. The clock struck nine as I gave my first yell.

Father heard me, heard the clock, thought that sounds like a boy and that clock's fast. He was right in both suppositions. More time had to pass before mother was aware of the first fact; the second she could never take in, not having her railwayman-husband's regard for the difference a minute makes. I think the happiest one present, for the moment, was Mrs. Crocker. She was so relieved, she thought me an absolute marvel to be alive. And when she discovered I had two crowns to my head, her triumph was complete—over my father, I mean. She pointed this out to him: 'He hes two croons to his heed, he'll be a prince.'

Yet after all I was a poor specimen, as my father was the first to point out. He also thought and said, very loudly, that my mother had nearly made a mess of the job, and he called the doctor a useless toy. The doctor was offended by that remark and left hurriedly, leaving my father free to go into the sick-room and put that clock right. At least, he'd start me running to time.

Chapter Two

A GREAT EXPLORATION—TANGLED
UP IN ASPIDISTRAS

I didn't do very well. I was no wonder-child like the first; nobody admired me. Small, ugly, ailing, and full of bad temper, that was my unpromising first appearance. My mother feared for my life; my father now and then pointed out that if she wasn't careful she'd lose this one, too; and the neighbours, who had so admired my sister but knew after she died that she was too beautiful to live, used to stop mother in the street to shake their heads over this poor baby. They'd peer into the pram (then called a go-cart to distinguish it from a push-chair, both better words than those we use now) and the crack generally was 'Oh, the poor thing, ye'll have a job to rear that one, Missus.' My only champion was the doctor, now reconciled because my father paid his bill on the nail and was in an unfortunate position argumentatively owing to Smuts and Co. having got reconciled to British rule. 'This one will live,' said the doctor. 'He's got a temper, he kicks against his troubles.' My mother, pleased, agreed, 'He's a little devil, got some of his father in him.' 'Ah, well, devils get on as well as angels in this world, often better—good morning.'

True, I kept them awake through many a night, dangling on my father's arm as he walked the floor with me and yelling down his tuneless rendering of 'Will Ye No Come Back again' or 'Oh, mama and dad, why couldn't you have had, your coon a different colour'. It seems to me that I even remember something of these occasions, so vividly do I recall a rolled shirt-sleeve, of thin stripes, pink, white and mauve, the fine skin and rolling muscles of his arm. One night when he thought I'd at last dropped off, I suddenly twisted and bit his thumb. He very nearly wrung my neck on the instant. But afterwards this incident gave him more respect for me, as one not so much ailing as wicked.

It is difficult to know at what point one can place early memories and begin to introduce them into a narrative which starts out of hearsay, actual evidence, so to speak and s'welp-me-God, which the subject of it can vouch for. There is an impression very far back, so far that I cannot remember when I first remembered it, of leafy branches moving slowly and with a regular undulation across bits of blue sky. Was this something seen as I lay in a go-cart and travelled gently along the paths of Heaton Park? Much too young, then, to remember, you think? I don't know. One of my pals, Laurence Bradshaw, can remember having his bottom blown on by a nurse, that being a fond habit of hers; and if Laurence's bottom can remember being blown on, why shouldn't my eyes remember being looked into by trees and sky?

There were great timeless, or nearly timeless, stretches in my young life then given over to Great Explorations, all in a little corner; Columbus-crawls to the many Indies and Americas in kitchen, scullery and backyard; by caravan to bedroom; or tottering on the long trail that led to the Forbidden Land of Front Room. All these territories were dotted with trophies from my mother's battles at the sales. The centre of life was the kitchen, a great ocean of linoleum from which sprang the legs of two tables, two chests of drawers, a sofa, and an armchair. The geography of these was more or less fixed. Other chairs with thinner legs and less secure frames were often in transit, sometimes combining so as to form a sort of maze not easy to thread one's way through. Then there was a black-and-blue rag mat, a hassock and a fender. These things I knew by touch, the chief of the senses early in life, the one to be more and more neglected later on. Less accessible and more tempting were the array of objects on the mantelpiece: a copper kettle, filled with a tangle of string, bootlaces and old keys; a copper iron-stand; a little milk-churn of polished brass; two nondescript vases; a calendar having a pouch bursting full of bills; and my father's watch, hanging on a nail always when he was off-duty. It wasn't long before I had all these pieces to play with, except the watch, and the control of them was more fascinating to me than playing with forgotten toys. The wall opposite was remote and less interesting. It carried three large pictures and a birdcage. The middle picture showed a jolly old gentleman in a fancy waistcoat, who held up a coloured handkerchief in his hand as he pointed at a parrot. In some lights this hand and handkerchief had the shape of a horse's head, a very horrible horse it was too, and sometimes I stared at it until it frightened me. But as I got older I learnt to switch it on and off—horse, handkerchief; handkerchief, horse—until all the terror had gone from it. The birdcage, near the window, held canaries, I believe, but all I remember now is being told that a canary once slipped out and flew straight into the fire. They might just as well let me have it. They wouldn't, though. Nor was I allowed to do much with the magnificent array of aspidistras and scented geranium which fringed that southward-looking window.

11

They made wonderful patterns of green light on the bit of floor under the clock—my favourite place for sitting on the pot. I must have looked a sort of gremlin child perched there directly under the clock, a green geranium-filtered light about me while the draught from the scullery-door on the other side froze my little bottom.

There were three steps down into the scullery, and half a dozen more to the back-door. From there, a long flight of harsh cement stairs went down to the back-yard, the lavatory (another of the silly words that have crept in), and the coal-house. Naturally, I wasn't allowed to travel that way on my own. My earliest excursions were mother-piloted. I remember only one of them before the age of two (you will read later why this was a crucial date). We were in a huge, high garden, mother and I, but I wasn't looking at her; I was looking down an expanse of long grass to where a couple of very tall ladies in long white dresses stood in front of a black summer-house and beckoned to me. I struggled through the long grass towards them, my feet catching, my mother behind me probably. It took a long time, but in the end I made it. The kind white ladies bent to me; one gave me a piece of Fry's Cream Chocolate in silver paper. I sat picking off the sparkling paper and uncovering the rich black-and-white inside while from the street below came a continuous noise of moving wheels and horse-harness jingling....

She must have taken me very often to the auction sales she was still so fond of because at the time they seem to have made a strong impression on me, even if it does not remain now. Apparently, I was very fond of playing by myself in the sacred Front Room—sacred, that is, in the general culture of the district, not so much so to my mother: she loved to use it because here reposed her chief trophies and she felt her cleverness congratulated by them whenever she had people in there. What a room it was, too, for a working-man's best! It was well-carpeted and well-lit. The chandelier hanging from the centre of an ornately moulded and plastered ceiling carried four large globes, though, mind you, it had to be a big occasion before all were ablaze at once. In fact, I remember it best under the silence of sunny afternoons. That sunshine was always diluted and aqueous, since the windows looked north, there was often a venetian blind hanging at the brightest and the others were half-obscured by white ochre-plastered lace curtains. A greenish, brownish, sea-weed-coloured light there, with motes in it and everywhere picking up reflections from many small mirrors in sideboard and overmantel and in the glass of many pictures. A sideboard faced the window and held two bronzes, vikings on prancing horses who waved

12

swords at their own reflections. On either side of it hung framed enlargements of wedding photographs, and in the recess by the fireplace stood a piano carrying more photographs. The tiled fireplace itself bore aloft an overmantel, all mirrors and brackets on which stood glass and china ornaments. There was a marble clock too, a presentation to my mother by her ex-colleagues in the jewellery business as you could read on a brass tablet under the dial. It was very impressive in front, a black Parthenon complete with columns at the sides and a frieze above; behind, though, as you saw its back reflected, it looked tawdry. The same mirror-squares and triangles reflected the wall opposite. A double row of oil paintings in heavy gold frames hung·from a rail upon a wallpaper of cream and silver streaks. Of course, the suite of furniture in it was plush, brown plush. My fingers still retain the touch of those chairs, so often did I trace round the carvings in the woodwork or try to draw designs on the plush by smoothing it all one way until it got light, and then rubbing one finger against the nap so as to leave a dark line. A solemn, plush-smelling room difficult to be gay in. But it got me into serious trouble all too soon.

There was a bay window to it in which stood a gate-legged table completely laden with an amazing collection of plant-pots, some of them in gilded china pots, some on saucers, and all holding up a dusty forest of aspidistras. Now one Sunday afternoon, in August, my parents were getting ready for a walk while I played quietly in the Front Room. Too quietly, it turned out. I was pretending to be an auctioneer selling aspidistras by lot. But the customers were a bit difficult, some liked the pots and not the plants, some the plants and not the pots. So, to make a deal of it, I offered to split the lots. That meant pulling the plants out of the pots, a messy operation. I was intent on it when my continued silence struck up suspicion next door. My father came in to see what was what, saw, flew into a rage and began thrashing me. I must have been badly frightened, or shocked at the sudden transition in my affairs, or perhaps he hit me too hard, anyway when my mother, who had been putting on her long, laced black boots, rushed to the rescue, I was blue in the face with what looked like a fit. Mother ran to get water, her long laces lashing about her ankles, while father followed carrying me. The three steps down into the scullery were her undoing: she tripped on the flying laces, slid forward, a foot under the mangle.

That put father in the right again, more or less, at least it put him in a fine fume of anger again which was almost the same as being in the right. He dropped me, and went to pick her up. I suppose I recovered. But she was hurt. Father wouldn't believe it. He made her walk up and down—'Try,' he ordered, 'go on, try, put your foot down.' She tried until she almost fainted from the pain, and still she couldn't. She wanted a doctor.

So father set off, his Sunday afternoon in ruins, his temper blowing away before a thundercloud of anxiety which his heartless behaviour was meant to hide. First he called at his brother Bill's place in the next street, to ask Aunt Mary Jane to come round, thus spoiling their Sunday afternoon. Mary Jane was all in favour of getting a doctor, naturally, she'd have been even more in favour of having a funeral there and then, if that was possible—the girl for the big event in a small circle, Mary Jane. But getting a doctor wasn't all that easy. Our own, the lad with the flowing beard, was on holiday; his locum was out. So was the next doctor, and the next. That exhausted Heaton Road, and left one hope: a young medico in a sidestreet. Swearing a lot, very warm and very impatient, my father collected this bloke and rushed him along.

He wasn't at all what the women had ordered. Something queer about him, they thought, was it drink? He diagnosed a broken ankle, and got ready to set it. But first he insisted on taking Aunt Mary Jane's measurements—she was then a very comely young woman. Odd behaviour. 'Nonsense,' said father, who had got his boots off and had very likely already taken Mary Jane's measurements himself, 'he set the thing, didn't he?' He did.

It wasn't right, though. When the plaster came off, mother still couldn't walk without a lot of pain. Our own doctor, now back on the job, had an X-ray photograph made—I remember finding a print of it, a grisly sheet showing something like the ghost of a demon pig's trotter. From it, we learned that the bones had not joined, there was a growth of ligament between. She went many times to hospital to see what they could do but from that unfortunate Sunday auction in the Front Room to the end of her life, she was a cripple.

Chapter Three

BEER AND MRS. BUCHAN

Well before this second of the train of disasters, which Grand-
mother prophesied, occurred, I had made my contact with
the community outside the home. In our street no babe was
allowed to stay entirely in its mother's care for long. Almost
before the tiny creature had settled in, deputations of small
girls would appear at the front door. 'Please, can I take the
baby out?' the eldest would begin politely, and then the
chorus came in, 'No, me, Mrs. Kiddar. Oh, let me, I'll be ever
so careful, and they'd pluck at her apron and stick themselves
as much in front of her as was humanly possible considering
the disparity in size. Now missus might be anxious as she
watched her precious sail off under the escort of a thin-armed
girl moving very gingerly and slow, but unquestionably baby
enjoyed it. The street was so full of grubby faces and hands
reaching in to pat his blankets and voices prattling comment
on his newness, he was King Baby as he moved up and down
in this dancing throng of new faces with ringlets and ribbons
to clutch, and comments for his every crow—it was a glorious
game this, and he the centre of it. Of course, it didn't last quite
like that. Presently he'd find himself parked for too long
beside a shop-window in which was the reflection of another
baby girl and a pram like his. He'd wait for the game to start
again. It didn't. Then he'd yell, and there'd be a perfunctory
shake or two of the pram: and if he kept on yelling, he'd
be stopped by a jerk that sent his little head back as the pram
made a bee-line for home, where mother, habituated by now
into making use of his absences, was busy blackleading and
couldn't take him up. 'Leave it by the railings, Beattie, I'll
bring him in when I've washed my hands,' she'd say, and dis-
appear. That was a facer, if you like, to be left belonging to
nobody after all that competition for his company when he
was new.

All the same when you could crawl and totter, you always
made for the street whenever the door was open. Over the
rough cement path, down the step onto the wonderfully
smooth pavement, perhaps on again to the cobblestones in the
middle of the road. As soon as you got into that dangerous
area, however, some little girl would come to lift you up and

15

totter with you back to safety. They were your street-guardians, the little girls. You were a nuisance to them when you crawled over the bays they had chalked out, or pee'd on them, or came too near their skipping-ropes, but they still accepted responsibility for you. I have one strong pavement-memory which must be pretty early. Summer again, and I was lying with my face close to the grey slate paving-stones tracing the cracks; they were as warm as dinner-plates; and there was a powerful, sickly smell of privet in blossom. Then drops like pennies came splashing down, patterning the light summer pavement with dark discs, and faster, wetting my hands, my hair, my back—I chuckled over the lovely pennies. No doubt I was lugged to shelter soon enough, and by a little girl, yet it was one of those moments, brief and trivial in themselves, for which time's clock stops. The only reason why they are indelible that I can see, is that in them everything stood still suddenly and all things were equally aware, not selecting, willing, making. Everything was in being, that only. And being is not transient.

The street was my second home. Though for some time mainly passive among its activities, I had the freedom of it by right and could come into its full heritage whenever I was able. That part I knew first, the south side, started with a grocer's shop on the corner, ran quite straight past some eighty front doors arranged in twos, one for the upstairs flat, one for the down, and each pair separated from the next by the downstairs garden. These gardens were just narrow fenders of soil laid round the buttress of the bay window but they were magnificently defended from depredation by low brick walls, coped with granite slabs each sprouting a complicated fence of spiked railings. The Edwardian builder imitated magnificence even in the cheapest house. Between them lay cement aprons in front of the doors. A lively youngster would often hop onto each of these in turn as he ran down the street, appearing and disappearing all the way down the pavement like something on a string. They were handy for the girls' games, too. Out of school-time, several of them would usually be in occupation as the various girl-gangs set up shops or schools in imitation of their elders. I got incorporated in these games, but not very cheerfully after the first time. It was wearing to have to sit still for a long time while Beattie Briggs waved a stick and put on an unpleasant voice with which to simulate teachers; and highly disappointing to have your favourite Nellie Potts lead you to a doorstep set out with empty cocoa tins and sugar packets so that it could call itself a shop and listen to a long dialogue about the price of bacon culminating at last in a series of buys which were mere

16

hollow pretence. I liked the boody-stalls best. Without warning some fine Saturday morning, and by one of those uncalculated and unpremeditated motions which sweep over child-communities, nearly every doorstep would begin to blossom in arrangements of broken glass, china and pebbles. 'Come and see my boody-stall,' Annie would call, and the late arrival on the scene would stand awhile admiring the treasure sparkling in the sun, the bits of blue glass, the pink and gold on a segment of china, the ancient sparkle of granite, the leaf gilded upon a lump of coal. Then the newcomer sped away to make her own collection—me helping perhaps: that's why I liked it.

But all these games could be abandoned at the sound of a bugle from the next street, and the cry which must follow: 'Rags, any ra-a-gs. Any jam-jars, any ra-a-gs!' At that, the small girl population vanished behind doors and I was left alone listening to the cry coming nearer. Not for long, though. One of the lasses was sure to be unlucky at home; she'd bethink herself of me and the unexploited reserves of my household. I'd be grabbed and hustled back to mother, to whom it was explained that I wanted some rags or jam-jars. By now, of course, the barrow was in the street, waiting, its paper windmills turning in the breeze. That's what you would get, a windmill made of rough stick and coloured wallpaper, or an umbrella of the same, or a fan, or a piece of pineapple rock. The older boys used to call out after the rag-man, 'Candy-rock for stocking legs, motor-cars for jam-jars', but we never got motor-cars. We returned to our occupations more or less equipped with our fancy and the bugle would be hard again in the next street and going away. Within half an hour or so, the rock was chewed up, the pretty wallpapers pulled off their sticks, and we were intent on something else.

The street was usually lively enough. These were the days of private enterprise; a mad economic maelstrom drew down every thoroughfare debris of competitive endeavour, such a procession of horse-drawn vans, man-pushed barrows, milk-chariots, coal-carts and steam-wagons as could have been achieved only by a separate deadly seriousness on the part of each participant blinding him to the comic glory he was collectively included in. Practically any moment of the day, one or other of these strange craft, ark or pinnace, was bound to come upon our horizon. The hooves of the faster traffic, doctor's trap or post-office van, shot sparks from our cobbles. Often there was a cry of 'Whip behind', and a couple of small boys would drop off the back and pick themselves up with bleeding knees and throwing sharp daring glances at any adults that might be about. The slower-moving door-to-door

17

tradesmen announced their presence: the milkman with a hand-bell and a high-pitched cry; the firewood seller with a long wail, 'D'ye wa-a-nt any sticks?'; the coal-man bluff, solid and low, 'coal ter wagon, coal ter wagon', and the hardware merchant, standing on his high cart, with a rapid ringing of plate against plate, produced an insistent tintinabulation which easily carried across several streets. Very often several of these were around at the same time, plus one or other of varieties of street musician, the tin whistler, the barrel-organist or the German band. With so many appeals on our air, so to speak, not only were we never quiet for long but as my mother said, 'You've got to keep your door tight shut if you want to keep a penny in your pocket, there's so many folks after it.'

And that was only the front street. Behind our houses, as was general in that district, ran the back lane. It was narrower, of course, with the same granite cobbles, smaller sidewalks, and monotonous brick walls pierced evenly along the whole length with two back-doors, two square openings into the coal-houses, two back-doors, and so on. Though milk and bread were front-door deliveries, greengrocery and fish and coal came to the back-door. Sometimes for days on end, the children would spend all their time in the back lane, in and out each other's yards, sitting on the steps, or swinging on the lamp-posts. Down here came the Cullercoats fishwives crying 'Caller Herrin' in that season and otherwise 'Fresh fish, hinny, straight from the sea'. They wore their traditional dress of dark-blue which so well set off the biscuit tan of arm and face, the salt-white hair, and they were like caryatids walking under the great baskets they carried on their heads.

Everybody's washing hung across the lane, so that the appearance of a tradesman's cart meant a rush to tuck sheets and things round the rope and to raise the diminished bunt-ing high over horse's head with a prop. The coal-man was the biggest menace, since a mere brush against his tarry sacks meant a second washing-day. At his cry every housewife instantly rushed out to struggle with the props, and down the lane you'd see one line of sheets after another shoot up a couple of yards and the horse's head appear very black beneath the sky-flung whiteness. Naturally bad lads learnt to imitate his cry. They'd conceal themselves behind the last line of washing, and give vent to a convincing 'Coal ter wagon!', then wait for the scamper.

Looking back, it seems I spent ages in these thoroughfares before I mustered enough small steam to move on my own motion to another street. Enormous summers dallied around

18

me as I sat on doorsteps or crawled about warm pavements always with the genial company of my kind close by. I belonged to that street by the same right that I had to belong to one particular family in it, and this social certitude stayed with me as it did with all of us, no matter what contemporary upheaval might be splitting our homes apart. All the livelong day, and it was a livelong day, I can tell you, whole man-months long, we were pavement-free and pal-pleasured. Home began again after such a huge interval, with the evening shouts of the mothers calling us in. Few took any notice of that, for a time, except to begin to feel uncomfortable; and presently there'd be a series of aproned descents, rushes, grabs, squawkings and the slam of another front-door. But often the lamp-lighter was on his rounds before all the small fry were safely back in their boxes.

My mother made no descents. For a long while she moved on crutches, and despite operations and visits to sanatoria for sea-water treatment, she was never again capable of making a rush at anybody. When we were out together, I thought it a great game to run ahead and hide. Peeping out, I saw her struggling along on the crutches, her face flushed with anxiety, her hat slipping over the heavy rolls of dark hair as the stumping of the crutches shook her, and when she paused, having quite lost me, I ran out at her full of clever glee. She was so afraid for me, for behind my antics she saw the bright ghost of her first wonderful baby that had twinkled so briefly and been whisked into nothingness for no reason she could see. An unlucky star stood over her, she was sure; she did not know what term there might be to its malevolence, whether it was already at an end, or if there'd come again the sudden clout of ungovernable calamity, aimed at her truly but through me. Much of her pleasure in me was spoilt by this fear. She was glad chiefly of the half-hour before my bed-time, when we were both safe before our own fireside, she could rest her permanently aching foot, and take pleasure in my eager response to the stories she told me. These were an interminable series concerning the adventures of Blackie and Whitie, two cats, told in her own pleasantly modified version of the Tyneside dialect, a singing speech-rhythm very apt to bedtime uses of all kinds.

Because stairs were awkward for her we had moved to the downstairs flat below, exchanging with our landlady, a widow, called Mrs. Buchan. I remember her well, and no wonder. She was the first of mother's new series of friends, all of them, without exception, menaces in one degree or another. Mrs. Buchan (in my mind, that is) was a female replica of Oliver Cromwell, padded out a bit. She was, perhaps, a bit lonely, and knew my mother was, so downstairs she came in the evenings bringing her sympathy and a jug of beer, to sit there making consolatory remarks of a heavy-sighing kind, 'Ah, well, there's nowt so bad but that it might be warse', and 'We all have a bitter cup to drink, hinny, it's poured out for us before we're born.' She'd slowly raise her own bitter drink, swing it over her high rampart of bosom, drink, lick the drop off a long whisker which usually hung from a corner of her mouth, and watch while the diminished glass travelled slowly over the battlements again. Then she closed her eyes, gave herself up I suppose to an inner savouring of the good that was being done her as the lovely drop of beer slowly percolated the immense ramifications of her figure. Presently the eyes would switch on; she was ready again for conversation and holding in reserve, you felt, the weighty comment to close it with. Sometimes you might think she was asleep. But she wasn't. She had slowly acquired a grave and monumental besozzlement, well contained in those stout corsets, and the content of it, the immense ease and nourishment it gave to all her flesh, kept her quiet for longer and longer periods. The last one, however, which came after the jug was empty, she'd abruptly end. A sharp twist of the head towards the clock, and she'd begin to call on her limbs to get ready, 'There now,' she'd say, 'time and tide'll wait for neebody, and neebody should wait for them—am to me bed.'

Meaning it kindly, I've no doubt, she introduced my mother to what she considered the fortifying influence of beer. My mother didn't like it at first, and took a glass only to be sociable, but soon enough she discovered it was an anodyne to pain. All day long she walked on the two ends of a broken bone separated by a ligament, and had little ease even when she rested; now in the evening, with her husband still at work and me put to bed, perhaps, she found Mrs. Buchan and her potion soothing company, out and in. But there was a snag to this which did not at first appear. She had no head for drink, or rather, since that is a damning statement to make about a near ancestor, her condition of pain and worry and disappointed hope so conflicted with the very nature of beer that its effect was to exaggerate her existing instability. Anyway, however one explains it now, at that time Beer and Mrs. Buchan got the blame for what followed.

If this was her story, it would be quite a job to trace the inroads and checks to the drink-habit which went on in the three years subsequent to her accident, but as it is mine, a few scattered memories may be evidence enough of what was happening and how, vaguely and fearfully, I was aware of something strangely wrong in our household. There comes to

20

my mind now, out of the long-ago confusion of those early years, impressions that don't seem to belong to me, not particularly. They loom like strange fish in an aquarium tank, becoming vivid briefly as they turn at the bright glass, and sink off with an effect of slow dissolution into the gloom and nothingness where they first took shape. I see, for instance— this sets the scale of my years—a vast beach of hillocky white sand, salt-bright on the crests, biscuit-colour in dimple and crater. People sprawl in groups; there is a lot of noise, dogs barking, shrill cries, the plunging splash and harsh sighing of waves, but over all, a voice calling 'Nougar, penny a bar!' I struggle towards the voice, my feet catching in the sand and huge dogs almost taking me off my legs as they tear past. There is a sort of rostrum painted in faded white and cracked yellow, above it a white jacket and a dark moustached face leaning towards me. . . .

It is late on a dark night, and mother stays in a glittering smoky shop with big brass doors by which I stand. People go in and out, passing me; one of them stoops to give me a new penny, but I am not happy. We are going home at last, and something is wrong with mother. She is flushed, her hat is falling off, she stumbles against her stick. She wants to turn into the back lane, which alarms me since its feeble gas-lamps have arcs of shadow trembling about them. She falls down and she cannot get up again. I stand crying for a long time. Then a man comes, the German pork-butcher from Heaton Road it is; he lifts her up; we lurch off into the gas-lit mottled dark. I mustn't tell father about this. . . .

Mrs. Buchan is with us, and we are standing outside a door at which a soldier stands yelling 'Early Door Gallery, Gallery this way', a woman in a shawl sells us oranges, and suddenly we are stumbling up a long staircase under lights in little cages; we see down below a fairyland of lit blues and pinks, and the fairies are real, they sparkle as they move; I am entranced and when the thing ceases after a final swoop of great red curtains, I want to know all about it and receive Mrs. Buchan's notion that it is Robinson Crusoe with scepticism. They disappear into the smoky glitter; after some peeping I go in boldly and seize mother's stick; some men laugh; we all come out. . . .

We are nearly home, in our own street, and again I know that all is wrong with mother; I talk to her incessantly, making sure I get answers; we get just inside our front door when she collapses; I pull at her and cannot move her a bit; she doesn't talk properly; I look along the dark passage and feel that the house has terrifying things in it; I conquer fear and move a little way towards the kitchen, hoping there may be a light in it; there isn't, and the shapes of old coats hanging on the wall are dusty-shouldered in the stray light from the street—they might be alive; I tug at mother, and she tries to rise; what does she say? Get the barber? The door is not quite closed; I squeeze through and run across to the barber opposite; he is just closing, and questions me over and over again before he'll come across and help. Mustn't tell father....

I am hungry, but mother lies helpless in the armchair; I pester her and she answers with an incoherent snore of broken words; I climb on a chair and get a tin of condensed milk from the table, take it to her; her hand grips it clumsily, she looks at it, and seems to listen to me now; her eyes close and she tilts the tin, slowly the thick condensed milk runs down the blue velvet dress over her breast, a great cream snot on the lovely deep-blue softness I loved so much. I am heart-broken. There is a sound of the key in the front-door—father!

Chapter Four

TRAVELS BEHIND A CLAY-PIPE

The appearance of the head of the household at the most awkward and unexpected times later became a recognized hazard in Kiddar life, but that time was not yet. In fact, during these earliest years my father played quite a pleasant role in my young life. I was impressed by his strange masculine power. He was big, of course; he was noisy; he was much stronger than any other person around. But it wasn't just that. He came out of another world and brought something of its atmosphere with him. My mother's opinions and doubts and worries, he simply overrode, as he did my own wayward-ness. She found herself under direct command to do some-thing, followed by a highly uncomplimentary remark if she didn't do it quick; me, I was swung up to an area of broad shoulder and hard bowler-brim where I had a lovely view of the street in the intervals when I was not blinking against the smoke and sparks from a clay-pipe. So we'd set out.

It was Saturday night, perhaps, and we were to go shopping in the town two miles away. I'd often made this trip by tram with mother, and she made an anxious business of it. She was afraid the tram would start off before we were fairly aboard; she was afraid every time we crossed a street, we'd be run down, a constant small panicking and fussing due to her lame-ness and to the lively imagination of those who have suffered irrational calamities. With father in charge, there was none of this. He expected trams and traffic to behave reasonably and so, of course, they did.

Whether it was the first call or not, we were bound to go into the Butcher Market sooner or later, a vast covered en-closure in which many sawdust-sprinkled aisles ran between the stalls not only of butchers but of booksellers, drapers, iron-mongers, cheap jewellers—glittering quicksands of proletarian penny-swallowing. The aisles echoed to the yells and yodels of salesmen, every one of them selling cheaper than the man next door. Mother, being a town-girl, thought she was a dab at buying well and always reckoned to save a copper or two on the weekly joint. Father, who came from the country, thought all the town-meat too long messed about and dear at any price. He had no patience with careful comparings and long

23

bargainings before you bought. All the same, for her sake, we stood a little aloof while she poked about and haggled, inhaling the butcher market smells, poultry, meat, and pipe-smoke predominating over an undercurrent of calico-dust, stale biscuit and damp sawdust.

I shared his impatience. I wanted to get to the Penny Bazaar quick, and it was in the next aisle not on the quickest route to the Flower Market which father would insist on taking if there was any more messing about. Not that he was liable to buy any flowers, of course. Pork sandwiches he was after. There again the different worlds of Da and Ma. Mother's expeditions often ended in a café called the Mecca because in her single days, already seen by her in the rosy glow of nostalgia, she used to go there for tea. They had a nice line in brown bread and butter—excellent, said she. I didn't see it. It seemed to me a pretty dim and female kind of fare, in no way up to the same establishment's cream cakes, yet such is the force of propaganda on the impressionable or of the true matriarchal wisdom, it is the brown bread I remember now, not the cakes.

However, being Dad-led, we were soon among the kiosks under the glass-roof of the Flower Market, making for a balcony where the odour of sweet decay from many damp and dying blossoms was crossed and then overwhelmed by the rich steam of roast pork. The sandwiches were made of round bread buns; they squelched rich gravy at you as you bit through to the thick pork and crackling within. My mother feared that this richness coming so late in the evening might upset a small boy's stomach—'Tommy-rot,' said father, 'if he can't stomach a bit of pork, he might as well turn his toes up now and not waste any more of folk's time.' So I set my teeth into the warm soft bun and tore corners off it. It never did me any harm. But to be fair to the female point of view, it was true that not for years did I eat the whole of one of these sandwiches. Father always finished first, ate what mother had left (which was usually more than half because she didn't really try knowing his need, or his greed, was greater than hers), and turned to me. 'Here you are,' he'd say, 'if you can't do better than that, I'll finish it for you.' And he did.

Having fed ourselves in this manner, some of us, the next move was to the Pineapple Grill for a drink. As I remember it his favourite drink was whisky with sugar and a slice of lemon. Its appearance often provoked him to tell an appropriate story. He'd look at his glass, the lemon rocking on the lovely gold and if it was a winter night a slight steam rising from the liquid, then he'd lean forward to address me but in his habitual loud voice which made all present turn towards us. 'D'ye know what the Frenchman said, after his first time in an

English pub? Ze Englishman, he says, 'e is mad. 'E orders a drink and 'ow must she come? Vy, zere is visky in it to make it strong, and vater to make it weak; 'e puts lemon in it to make it sour, and sugar to make it sweet; zen 'e says " 'Ere's to you," and drinks it 'imself.'

This always got a laugh or a smile, particularly from any women that were present, as present they would be in such a pub as the Pineapple. They always warmed easily, you see, to my father's noble proportions and handsome looks which gave his wit a female-penetrating quality wit, on its own or in the wrong mouth, is so liable to lack. Because of that audience, or anyway, mother didn't like this tavern forwardness of his. So she said, but, maybe, it was just her cue to be gently deploring at such times—showed she owned the animal. Myself, sitting small on a slippery settee balanced by elbows uncomfortably high on the beer-smelling table, enjoyed it well. The blood of a thousand drinking ancestors rejoiced as my senses recaptured for it familiar excitations of sight, sound and smell. Yes, I took up a portion of the communal glow about and was enhanced.

Of course, father's drinking was different. He didn't flush, stumble over words, or fall down helpless. All that happened as the whiskies twinkled away towards their natural Valhalla, was that the raw edges of his awkward temper wore down. He became almost genial, and, in flashes, even considerate. He was very much all right, and in his charge we came home happily in the shaky old trams which sparked their way over the wind-clutched Byker Bridge.

There were Sunday mornings, too, which father's aegis gave an interest to. All his interventions were rare and intermittent, since the distant whirlpool of railway work sucked him away very often at those times other men, with different jobs, are able to spend with their families. Yet I remember him on some Sunday mornings at least, making breakfast while mother and I lay in bed—it stays in my mind, I think, because it was such an unlikely act of domestic tenderness for him to perform and in after years no one would have believed he would do it. It happened, though. The wonderful morning smell of frying bacon heralded the approach of his heavy steps; mother and I hastily stuffed pillows behind our backs; and in he came in bearing a large black tray, patterned in red flowers, on which stood a far bigger breakfast than we usually got.

Occasionally again he took me for a Sunday morning walk. Generally I seemed to be ill on these occasions—I was often ill up to the age of seven—and he was no fit companion for the sick. He'd never been ill in his life, not a day nor an hour;

25

he just didn't know what illness was about. We'd walk the hot, red paths of Jesmond Dene, brick-red gravel dust throwing the heat up into my inclined face, and the tiresome rich green of full summer seeming to shout at one to look, look up, look around. I swayed on in the grip of a huge, hot fist being pulled out of the way of swaying sickly-scented skirts and around the sharp shine of polished boots. 'Sit down,' I repeated whenever I had the strength to say it, 'sit down.' But father was a man of trains and punctually-achieved destinations: he had a seat in mind, and it was high up one of the steep paths leading to Paddy Freeman's pond. When he saw I couldn't make it, he picked me up—a bit bothered, mind you, because he thought me getting on to be a big boy now, and he wouldn't accept my mother's idea that I had a weak chest. My mother's idea —she had my chest smothered in cotton-wool and some unpleasant oil or other, and the prickly heat of it could have driven me mad if I'd had the strength to be anything more than miserable. I tore and scratched at it when at last we sat down by a little stagnant pond. The water there was of a tarry blackness where it showed through a green-gold scum, the surface like Chinese lacquer with here and there the evil wink of too-bright sunshine—it swam before my eyes as I looked at it....

I don't suppose these trips were a great success, but in one matter, father and son were united. We developed a mutual love of comic papers, and together taught ourselves to read them. He could read after a fashion before I arrived, it's true, for once he'd struggled all the way through a serial in the *Girls' Own Paper* called *The Shepherd's Fairy*. But he was poor at the accomplishment and too touchy to be improved by help from others. With me, now, uncritical of pronunciation and eager for the gist of the tale, he could hold forth confidently, skipping the tangled bits. He sat always in a hard chair, right-hand side of the kitchen range, with his back to the window, his sleeves rolled up and the paper held firmly. There were no arms to his chair, so he never lolled. Then, being set, off he'd go into the latest crime of Jasper Todd, the sinister landlord of the Red Inn, or of Spring-heeled Jack, or the ingenious interventions of George Gale, the Flying Detective. I stood with one hand on his corduroy knee, with the other waffing away the fat layers of fawn-grey smoke which lay like phantom rashers in the sunlight twisting into nothingness as his pipe went out for the umpteenth time and I was impatient to see him pause for a re-light. Mother bustled about us with pans and things, now and then cleverly correcting his pronunciation. 'No, not lethargy, letharjy, man.' 'Shut up, Ma', I'd say quickly, and we went on until every item in

26

Chips, Comic Cuts, Lot o' Fun and the *Butterfly* had been dealt with—for that week.

One day, however, I made a discovery. I could read myself! I was four years old now, I suppose, thin, rather weakly, too feminine in appearance for the taste of the local matrons but undeniably bright; and while sprawling on the floor with a comic open at the pictures of Weary Willie and Tired Tim, or Dreamy Daniel, or Casey Court, or the Mulberry Flatites, I found that the captions under suddenly began to read themselves out to me. Marvellous! Mother, when she learned of this, was pleased and proud: it justified her somehow. Father probably was not so pleased; it must have seemed to him something in the way of *lèse-majesté* that a mere babe should jump into a faculty himself had acquired so late in life, an uncanny forwardness that boded no good. He mentioned his doubts to Granny. Her ruling was that the Kiddars were an unaccountable clan in any case, much given to surprising folks; and that her youngest son was also one who took to the printed page at an age when he should have been running about with the other lads; in short, such things were in the breed and must out, here and there among the progeny.

This grandmother, that is my father's mother, had recently become a factor in my life. She moved into our district after her husband's death to an upstairs flat in Chillingham Road, opposite the school. With her was this same youngest son, Robin, whose eccentricities were often to be my exemplar. A small woman to have such big sons, you'd think, small but hard as a nut, her will trained in long association with an easy-going philosophical husband and in effective rule over a family of four sons and three daughters. By the time I came along to see her, she had weakened, at any rate as regards grandchildren, who were not her prime responsibility and could be pleasured in with that delicate, second phase of maternal feeling which belongs to grandmothers. I was welcome and I liked her house. There was something pleasurably impermanent about it, as though she was on the move from one country cottage to another taking a few precious properties with her. There was an oak desk bureau, which had arms you could pull out. I pulled and as the arm shot out, a ha'penny fell from it—magic! But you had only to do that once or the magic would be broken. There were peacock feathers in a corner, and the great eyes of them dilated and contracted as you moved round the room. Sometimes, I was given one to take home with me. Then for the next few days I marched with it to fairylands long forgotten now. There was a great picture of a man in long robes who wore a crown of thorns and carried a lantern—that was Jesus, I was told, but I didn't believe it, not in Granny's house it couldn't be. It was some mysterious Other they weren't willing to tell me the name of for one of those curious adult reasons. And there was the boat. Looked at with an ordinary gaze, it was a model of a three-masted schooner, all correct in planking, rudder and holds, though with the masts missing, and huge—well, about two foot nine long actually, but enlarged in story. Many times as I sat playing with it, Granny's voice described the Argo voyages we were to make in it some day, just her and I, and her slow country speech in the dialect of over the Border people mistakenly call Scots, had a touch of the foreign in it which made her promises of far journeying all the more convincing.

Then one day she went. 'Granny's gone', they told me. Instantly I thought of the boat; I wept to think that they'd gone without me. They showed me the boat; they even gave me the boat to take home with me and be my own. But now it was a shabby thing, one of its planks sprung loose from the bows, no sails, dead, useless, its magic passed away. Nevertheless, there it was, and Granny gone. I suspected that Holman Hunt figure they pretended was Jesus: he with his lantern had shown her the secret ways down the sky-slopes at the back of the moon. If it wasn't so why did they keep the front room door locked, eh? Because he wasn't in there any more.

My father settled all this nonsense by taking me into that room and showing me Granny. She lay in her coffin, a larger boat than mine was, her face frilled round with linen, and looking like a wax crab-apple, quite unreal. It was magic, but bad magic; I didn't understand it at all. The mystery objectified itself on my shocked imagination and became a recurrent nightmare.

I was five now, sleeping alone in the room immediately below that where I was born. There had been changes in the layout of the household owing to the arrival of a baby sister. The precious front room was a bedroom now, complete with an enormous brass bed having both canopy and side-curtains —a bastard if ever there was one—in which my parents slept, and a cot for the kiddy. So I was banished to sleep alone and nightly lay staring at the great window giving on to the back-yard. Its panes were blank and dark enough, lord knows, they showed you nothing but the gusty blackness a couple of stars struggled to be borne on, and momentarily, the sudden brimming of blue light when an electric train passing in the gully beyond the opposite houses ground on the live rail. Yet it was the last my eyes saw before slumber had me, and when I slept, I was soon awakened (as I thought) by the mad hooting of an owl, at which the great figure of the Crowned Christ

28

stepped into the window, filling it with colour and with the urgent yellow rays of the lantern—it beckoned, it stood and beckoned. I howled with terror. Not till that winter had worn itself out, was I safe from this visitation, and it was many years later before I'd ever trust myself to say what it was used to frighten me so much, or why it was such a mad howl I set up instead of the usual fretful crying of lonely children.

Chapter Five

A ONE-EYED GUNNER KICKS

My sister was born three weeks before my own fifth birthday, and my mother was fearful of her coming because, as she said, her own lameness might have marked the child. But that was only to give a reasonable reason to people who naturally scouted her belief that she was marked down for calamity and might expect its appearance in any of Life's contingencies. All the same she must have impressed her secret faith on the neighbours since they believed my report after I'd seen the new baby. Someone asked, after hearing it was a girl, what colour its eyes were. 'Yellow,' I said, with certainty, that being my favourite colour at the time. So once again, the cry up and down the street was 'Poor Mrs. Kiddar, what luck that lass always has.'

Now actually the new baby was no calamity at all. Right from the start, and continuing, she was a contented pudding of a kid that ate and slept and stayed put just as ordered. She added a bit of ballast to the household which was needed. My father even had hopes that at last somebody had arrived who might be expected to show a bit of ordinary good sense about the business of living. When you gave her food, she ate; when you played with her, she chuckled; when you laid her down in a cot or a pram, she slept—no bother at all with our Lilian.

She was even a bit of a blessing to me. With her around the folks didn't bother so much about me; and that was all right because I was five now, at the end of my infancy and ready to go to school. Or so I thought. And duly on a bright summer morning at the end of the holidays, my mother set out with me to have my name enrolled as a scholar in the local elementary school.

The school was only a few streets away, within the Avenues. There were ten of these, of which ours was Third, all built in one plan though not by any civic authority. The First and Third ran parallel to the railway lines, sharing a common back lane; three short ones, and back lanes, were at right angles to the rest, but extended only from third to Seventh; Seventh, Eighth, Ninth and Tenth were parallel, too; and the long Second ran at right-angles to the railway from it as far as Tenth, though where it was not keeping the short avenues company, it was all corner-ends owing to the interruption of the lanes and front streets that ran into it. To make room for the school buildings, half of the north side of Ninth and the south side of Tenth was missing. Our route that fine morning then was across Third into Fifth, down Seventh as far as the back lane to Chillingham Road (that being the fourth side of the square); along the lane past end of Eighth, and into Ninth. Well, there we were.

Well, not quite. I jibbed at the sign over the door which said Infants. I was five and no infant. My mother, with that pliability which so often got her into trouble, allowed herself to be dragged round to the Tenth Avenue entrance which said Boys. This was it, I thought, undoubtedly. But mother hesitated about going in. Presently we were spotted from afar by a caretaker, a fellow with a bristling moustache and an aggressively well-washed blue work-jacket. The moment he spoke, I realized he was one of my father's make: no moving him. 'Ye don't want to be in here at all,' he said, with utter emphasis. 'That boy's an infant. Go round the back to where it says Infants on the door, plain for all to read.' And he watched us off that part of the premises with a sort of contemptuous relish, being obviously a student of human folly, feminine section especially.

At length I was duly deposited among my contemporaries, a class of some fifty children, more than half of them girls I was disgusted to note. It was a very pleasant class-room, though. The morning sun shone in through wide windows over blue glass vases and painted pottery jugs holding flowers on to the yellow desks; it made a sort of fuzzy incandescence out of the ends of the little girls' pigtails, and even struck a dull china gleam from the celluloid Eton collar worn by nearly every boy. I was impressed by the teacher, too. She was a lady, not so much for the way she dressed, the long black skirt, full-frilled blouse going up to a high lace collar supported with whale-bone struts was regulation Edwardian, but because she talked posh. All day. I'd heard the little girls imitating her, of course, but these were unnatural and not very prolonged performances. It hadn't occurred to me that anyone could keep up that kind of lingo constantly and with ease. Her name was Miss Greensill and I admired her at once.

But not for long. We were given brushes and little porcelain dishes containing water-colour, or else coloured straws which we were supposed to plait—babyish stuff, but not too bad. Then there'd be a lesson. A cracked yellow scroll was unrolled and hung on the blackboard. It showed three-letter words, and very fat black letters they were, spaced out and then put together. Teacher took a long pointer, touched each

31

letter in turn, and said, 'Kuh, Ahh, Tuh spells Cat.' The class intoned cheerlessly, 'Kuh, Ahh, Tuh spells Cat.' The pointer moved down a line—'Muh, Ahh, Tuh spells Mat.' The class dutifully chanted after her. Then teacher got clever. 'Ruh, Ahh, Tuh—' she stopped. 'What does Ruh, Ahh, Tuh spell, Freddy?' Freddy got to his feet and threw a hapless glance down at the girl next to him. 'Please, teacher, Ah divn't knaa.' 'You mustn't say "divn't", say "I don't know". Though you ought to know that little word the times you've heard it. Can you tell him, Elizabeth?' Bright Bessie rattled off, 'Ruh, Ahh, Tuh spells Rat, teacher,' but Freddy didn't look as if he was taking any notice of her.

I must say a little of this was quite enough for me, too. I could read quite well, but I read whole words, and quite unconsciously for their sense; I had never bothered with this curious dismemberment into Tuhs and Buhs and Ahhs. It seemed to me to make the whole thing most irritatingly difficult.

However, they had story books in the cupboards and when these were dished out, my hopes rose. Being a newcomer, I was told just to look at the pictures. I did, and then I read the damn thing. It was all about some over-infantile children who went to a farm and had such fun pointing at the animals. Not a murder, not a fight, not one horrible character to freeze your attention; and the writing was a sort of baby-talk anyway. I went drearily through the pages and back again until I knew every illustration by heart and could be sick in advance at the sight of the next one coming up, then it was next lesson. What was this going to be? Singing—Jesus wept, I said under my breath, using one of father's forbidden phrases.

A few days of this and I had acquired the one faculty with which every school infallibly endows its pupils, that of being bored. It is very important, of course, that every child should in the course of time become fitted up with this negative capability. If they didn't have it, they'd never put up with the jobs they are going to get, most of them, on leaving school. Boredom, or the ability to endure it, is the hub on which the whole universe of work turns. The genius and the chimpanzee are impatient of it, and here and there in a civilized society occur individuals who hark back to these ancestral types and are resis'nt to scholarship. Their subsequent careers vary. They may be kicked about and generally deplored like the genius, put behind bars like the ape, or supposing they manage to combine the two acts and show the public chimpanzee playing genius, or genius playing chimp, then they get applauded as Great Personalities. Most of us, however, are unable to survive being educated. We learn reading and boredom, writing

32

and boredom, arithmetic and boredom, and so on according to curriculum, till in the end it is quite certain you can put us to the most boring job there is and we'll endure it.

I managed one small kick against this educational system before it got the real half-Nelson on me. There was a lad a little older than myself I was delighted to chum up with, because his name was Ben and he only had one eye. One of father's yarns concerned a one-eyed gunner—well, here he was, a one-eyed gunner just my size. I took him home with me in triumph. Father saw the point and was ready with his chuckle but mother was quelling: somehow the very phrase 'one-eyed gunner' disappeared out of the family lingo.

Ben was still about, though. One morning, going to school, I came across him. He sat on the kerb, poking around with a bit of wire in the grate. Various dollops of filth were coming up, but the prize he was after, a small door-key, eluded his efforts. I got a bit of stick to help. It was quite ineffective, but it got me in the game. We poked away very happily until a curious spread of hush about the street made me aware that the school-bell had stopped ringing.

'Howway, Ben,' I said, 'we're late.'

I know I must have said these words, terrible though they sound on the lips of one just out of infancy, for I had been to school and knew this much already, that the golden rule of the perpetually-bored is Punctuality.

'That place, huh! Huh, ohh, tuh.' Ben grinned up at me, and then resumed his poking. 'Ruh, ohh, tuh,' he said to the grating, 'tommy ruh, ohh, tuh.'

Of course, Ben was right, one-eye or no one-eye; I would stay with him. The thing wanted some managing, mind you, since the folks at home certainly wouldn't approve. It was easy, so Ben said, you had to be careful to keep out of the way of everybody during school-sessions and turn up at home when they were over. That's why he generally went to the park.

I went with him, and for the next few weeks we lived in glorious freedom, frayed only at the edges by our necessary home-comings and the lies you had to tell when you got there. 'What have you been learning today?' 'Oh, reading and writing,' you said gruffly, feeling the twinge of conscience.

During this period, but very near its end, there was an early fall of snow. Ben and I were delighted. We plunged into this white and muffled world, snowballing street-lamps and back-yard doors as we went, dodged between the stumbling horse-traffic of the main road, and were a couple of Robinson Crusoes in the unspotted wilderness of the park. It was fun to print our footsteps over the glimmering level that had been a bowling-green, the very first men on a new-made moon. We

33

shouted up at the beeches, our voices having an odd tinkling quality against the snow-veils and sometimes bringing down a heavy crest to plump into the bushes and startle a blackbird into scampering flight like a blown rag on the snow-dazzled air.

Presently we heard other voices. They came from over the hill, with them a low trundling sound which could only mean one thing: the sledges were out. Of course, these were being run by quite big lads, youths no less, either absent from work or unemployed. Ben and I must humbly stand and watch. But for sledging, if the sledge is big enough, you want to load up. We were small fry, but we made one; separately we got included among the august. It scared us stiff, I may say. The hill was broad on the top, the runners moving uncertainly after the kick-off, but as the ground fell away there was a gathering swoop, faster till the air whistled and bent in upon us, the sledge leapt to a swelling ridge, we fairly shot towards the trees, swerved, braked and flattened out in a wide crunching arc, curving round and slowing into the soft snow of the bottom levels. This was great, may it go on for ever!

Actually it went on for a few days. Then something went wrong. Some milder air blew up during the night, snow-bergs slid and crashed from the roofs, the gutters ran water and were choked with slush, between the old piles of snow from the pavements each cobbled road was a river flowing over hammered ice-sheets. My pal Ben did not appear. After plodging about for an hour or two, I had wet feet; I was oddly disheartened. Home drew me like a criminal to the scene of his crime. I didn't go there, but I drifted to the vicinity, getting as far, or rather as near, as the pub at the end of our street. My idea was to see the time, if it said I could return as from school yet. By climbing on the railings of the forecourt. I could see the clock in the Chillingham Hotel. I pulled myself up out of the slush, and was getting on tip-toe to see when a huge familiar figure appeared behind me. My father, coming off shift, his bait-tin under his arm, knew at once I'd been 'playing the wag', as he called it. However, he collected me with his free arm and bore me off home, nothing much said so far.

This was by no means the end of it, no, in fact, there was a regular jumping-jack trail of consequences to our truancy. The authorities had been taking note of it quietly all the time. Now they summoned father to appear before a School Attendance Committee, or some such. There some bright little man, hard inside with the boredom of his own upbringing, gave it as his opinion that I needed discipline. Discipline, why certainly, all agreed to that. Discipline, oh yes, blessed stuff

34

that even the meanest ever to get in a position of authority are always ready to give away with both hands. Discipline, nod, nod, social cement—stick it on the rebellious till they stiffen. Well, then, summed up the bright little man, we may overlook this case providing the boy's father proves he is capable of applying discipline by giving the boy a severe thrashing— would he promise to do that? My father at that moment was very much in a mind to give all present a severe thrashing, and was extremely capable of doing it. Perhaps they guessed something of his temper. At any rate they bothered him no more after he'd said that he'd see the laddie went to school in future.

I got my thrashing, nevertheless. It was severe, but that didn't matter. It was cold-blooded, unprovoked, and carried out by a man whose unease was not the heat of anger nor anything that my small experience recognized, so there was a shock in it. Mother returned shortly after it was all over, and she, I think, felt betrayed. The man is dangerous. We both were chary of looking at him. He sat in his usual place by the fireside, strong, clean and smiling, but wrong, utterly wrong inside. He had blacklegged his own best impulse, and for such as he, blacklegging of any kind, not rebellion, is the major crime.

Ben disappeared, never more to be seen. Apparently, he had no father to administer discipline—in fact, there was some mystery about his domestic circumstances. I remember vaguely that his mother was a beautiful lady who once wept over him, he scowling out of his one eye ... and that's all. But I believed he'd been sent to the training ship which later got quite a number of my pals as ripening years magnified their natural delinquencies.

However, mother and I set out for school once more. Her idea was to persuade the teacher to make me a monitor, so as to give me an interest. Teacher agreed, and I started there and then on my new duties. These consisted in dishing out and re-collecting books, slates and the china water-paint platters. I had to take these last to the wash-basins and clean them. Of course, I knocked off a few just to show the street I wasn't bought over, and then settled down to the life of punctual attendance and pretended industry which was the normal surface to show at school.

All the same, and both for good and for ill, I had learnt and retained something from this experience of truancy which not all the children of eternity doing their stretch of time are able to know. By self-inflicted outlawry one can regain a world relatively innocent of the ticking clock and of the measured out values, human and material, that tick is the

35

ready symbol of. You can fall out of step, you can question any general obedience, by no more elaborate strategy than an obstinate boldness. True, you will certainly be punished for this, if only by a powerful and disheartening disapproval. You may also be rewarded, distantly and doubtfully. The point is, that for the period of your freedom, you have been an outsider to whom the contrived universe of the socially-included is a curiosity. Afterwards, its compulsions will always lack the final validity; you'll be prepared to see them varied, or to advocate their disuse; you'll keep somewhere in you, a useful incredulity which is really a readiness to welcome the coming of livelier customs that haven't had the spring worn out of them by the bottoms of the sit-pretties.

Of course, I had no sense of any such then. For five days a week as far as one could see down the years, my own little bottom was to squirm on a form, my elbows dig into a desk, during the most golden hours of the day. In this position I was often very happy, it's true. I was with my mates, shared with them in collective naughtiness; the teachers often brought out something of real interest to a growing lad; and now and then delightful things happened. They gave us *Coral Island* to read. I took it home and went through it one week-end. Then we read it painfully, one by one, in class. I couldn't help but read it again, and again, rather than listen to the stumbling recitation of Freddy Tingall or Bill Snowden or the affected rattle of Lizzie Heslop. Even then I still enjoyed it. But when we started a new term, there was no new book, no; we were to go through *Coral Island* again. And that, hell's bells, was a sentence.

Out of school, I was beginning to graduate as a corner-lad. It was my baby sister now who was the pride and anxious delight of the girls. I sometimes roughly asserted my prior relationship to her, but far more often was to be seen hanging about the corner-end in hopes of being included in the big boys' sports. According to the incidence of boy-population about half the corners had their own gangs. I drifted for a time between two of these, Third Avenue, which had its customary headquarters round Daddy Hilton's grocery at the bottom, and Sixth Avenue who congregated at the barber's window right opposite our house. Second could never call a corner its own; Fifth was too short of boys; Fourth had a gang, but they were weak and swamped with their own girls; Seventh were a numerous and lusty lot of thugs; and the rest were too far away to be my concern yet awhile.

The youngest member's position was far from enviable. He was included only in such games as needed a lot of players and would not be spoilt by his inefficiency; he was left behind

36

on all the more important expeditions, and in local exploits was generally the one to be caught and clouted by the adult they were plaguing. If he sat quiet, he might listen to much brave talk and big boys' wisdom, but when they were bored he easily became the sport of kings, was mildly tortured and ragged, and perhaps sent home weeping. In the marble season, he never held his marbles for long; the big lads won them from him. The same happened to his cigarette cards, known locally as 'crests'. Even if he was merely eating an apple, there was bound to be some great lout hanging over him waiting for the core, and deploring every bite he took with outcries and appeals until he yielded it up. Yet all this was nothing beside the tremendous goodness of belonging to the élite of his street.

I went to the corner immediately after tea, and could be prised away from it at bedtime only after many appeals. 'In a minute, Ma,' I'd yell back testily, hoping the other lads noticed how independent I was. Sometimes they would order me home themselves, thinking it was cheeky of me to want to stay out as late as they did. As long as I could, though, I stayed. The marble millionaires gambled untold wealth at Big Ring, increasing the stakes as the evening wore on until there was a fortune out there on the cement, whole constellations of fat milkies and coloured glass-alleys with twinkling spirals down their centres and clear sea-green or water-white pop-alleys winked in the shaky gaslight, nothing less than these high counters allowed in the big game, stonies and chalkies definitely barred. Then in came the bullocker shot from the ringside. The constellation shook and was scrambled; single stars fled or rolled towards the chalk ring. All that went over belonged to the lad ·that made the shot. Sometimes, none did. Right, next player. The winners dropped their captured beauties with a happy plonk into the poke they nearly all carried; losers might fish for a last treasure, a broken pen-knife or a watch-compass, to barter for another stake. There were no quarrels, since the only dispute could be whether a marble was, or wasn't, over the line, and there was an automatic majority against the two who each stood to profit by argument.

It wasn't always marbles. Other games came along in their own season. There were even idle evenings when the lads simply sat yarning and speculating about life, particularly the life they would have when they left school and were real working-men. I liked these nights best, though, of course, I sat silent and usually a little out of the light coming from the shop-window or the street-lamp. They would discuss ways of becoming strong, whether the chewing of calamos root really did assist one's wind; how many times a day one could masturbate without going mad, and were masturbators weakening themselves or expressing a natural virility; what job was the healthiest; whose dad was the strongest (here I had my moment of pride, since mine was certainly the biggest) whose was the best scrapper, then; boxers in general; how does a man get knocked out; why does a woman faint; how does she get pregnant; if a passionate girl goes with a virile man who is the first to have had enough; will the present company marry when they grow up; what will the same do with their money when they are working; what's the value of beer to a man; is it proof of strength to be able to drink a lot; do certain kinds of work make beer-drinking imperative; is it better to be your own boss in a small way or one of the blokes; and, very late on, murders and ghosts.

Most often I was called away at an interesting point, but I never made the mistake of asking my mother any questions. She'd have been horrified to know of some of the stuff I'd heard; and Lord alone knows what sort of job she'd have made of it if she'd had to explain sex to me in the way the modern parent is supposed to, a way that must surely be womanish and school-teacherly and too allusive to cover the matters of continuing male virility and dangerous female vitality which are really the essence of the whole thing. But just as I switched school out of my mind when I came into the street, I shut out the street with its door and looked for my supper.

On the subject of suppers, mother and I were agreed. We both liked best those she didn't have to prepare herself. So when she was in funds, I'd be given a jug and sent off to the corner shop to get two penny pies and a penn'orth of peas; or run along to the fish-and-chip saloon for a penny one and a ha'porth twice, please. If broke, we'd do roast potatoes or have an onion cut up in vinegar. Whatever it was, we disposed of it very quickly; and then I'd begin slowly and unwillingly getting ready for bed, making immense pauses between the removal of each garment and putting in a remark now and then to keep her talking. Of course, she thought I ought to be in bed; every now and then she made an effort to get me there. But she was lonely on the long nights when her husband was at work and moved by such a nostalgia for the days when she was unmarried, uncrippled, moving in a bright and busy world, that she was glad to talk of this fading past even to such a poor audience as me.

She pulled her chair well into the fire, pulled up her skirts to give her knees a warm thus showing black stockings gartered below the knee with bits of old ribbon or bootlace and black boots laced up to support the broken ankle. When her

38

skirts warmed they smelt of piss. This was not at all unusual among Edwardian females, by the way. I suppose ladies' lavatories were scarcer, or, perhaps, the long skirts of the period encouraged the easy yielding to the promptings of the bladder, anyway it was a frequent encounter if you were a small boy, to come into a quiet back-lane and find a lady apparently lost in thought. Her eyes surveyed the roof-tops or looked without purpose into the distance—was she listening to that muffled splashing? She certainly took no notice of the dark stream appearing under her boot, and when you came closer to see what it was—'Go away, boy,' she'd say, starting from her dream. Any other woman passing by would also turn on you; you were hustled off like a rebuked puppy, conscious of having offended, but not knowing wherein the offence lay. Such episodes left traces on the long skirt.

Mother generally played with a poker, perpetually touching grate or fender as she told of the balls she'd been to and how pretty all said she was, rather like an ex-Cinderella whom the Prince had discarded in early middle-age and who sat at a hopeless hearth now, forlorn of fairyland. I did not appreciate what these distant triumphs were. For me, the interesting part of her life was when she was a little girl. I'd ask the right question at the right time, and off she'd go. 'We were poor, mind, sometimes so poor mother didn't know where to turn to even for a bit of food for us. When Da got a job, do you know what she'd do? She'd go to a sale and buy a sack of rice or a sack of flour, and when we saw what she'd got, we'd say, "Oh, Ma, whatever do you buy that stuff for?" "You'll be glad of it before long, see if you aren't." She was right. You see, our poor Da would start drinking again, he promised he wouldn't but he was such good company with his singing and the funny things he said, the fellows would make him drunk for fun. Then he'd get the sack. Every week after that we were harder and harder up, oh, you've no idea how poor we were. Less and less to eat, until mebbe there was only rice left, and it was rice every day, boiled rice, no milk, not much sugar. Eh, when I hear how the poor Indians live I'm sorry for them, 'cos I know what it is. Often we thought our mother was a hard woman, but she had to be, she'd never have brought us all up if she hadn't been. Us girls were all eager to help her as soon as we were old enough—d'ye know what I used to do? I used to go out to light Jews' fires on the Saturday morning. You see, Willie, Saturday is the Jews' sabbath, like our Sunday, and they are not allowed to do any work, not even lighting fires. So I used to go round from house to house, as many as I could. But I was just a little girl and sometimes the fires wouldn't burn up, not if I blew till my cheeks were like big apples.

The Jews would get impatient—they could light them better themselves of course, if it wasn't for their religion—they'd say things in their language. Eh, some of them were good to me, though; I always had some coppers for my pains. Oh, I used to be so proud, running into our house and saying, "Here you are, Ma", never no more than that as I put the pennies into her hand.'

She'd sigh, and swing the poker gently against the bars of the fire. 'Ah, well, it's little the poor gets, and a little does them good.'

Some such curtain-line often brought the session to a close. Bed next, a final 'Good-night and God bless' taken unwillingly by me, somehow, and I was left to darkness and the night-stare of the great black panes. Presently, however, the lights went on in the little theatre of my imagination; I saw the scene, as it might be in a panto, the shabby little girl puffing away at a small flame, its light flickering up on the circle of Jews, all with hooked noses and black forked beards who muttered in a strange language and made helpless gestures with hands tied by religion. Perhaps late on, I'd hear a key turned in the front-door lock, and my father's heavy stumbling steps along the dark passage. This was reassuring. One could sleep safe if he was here.

Chapter Six

GRANDMA'S GOD AND
RAILWAYMAN'S RIGHTS

There were, of course, many evenings and some Sundays on
which the regular routine of the railway allowed my father
some freedom. At first, it was the Sundays which chiefly
interested his family. His edict would go forth: all to be ready
by two o'clock. My hope always was that we were going to the
seaside, as rarely we did, but it was much more likely that our
destination was Grandma's, a longish tram-ride away into the
centre of the city. This was Grandma Johnson, mother of
my mother and a very different proposition from the other
old lady who deserted me for a mysterious journey I could
have no part in.

Her house epitomized her life. She lived in Bath Lane
Terrace, hard by the Brewery and opposite a very dead little
shop which let out invalid chairs on hire. A highly-respectable
street this, particularly on Sundays which was when I most
often saw it; three steps up to each pair of downstairs and
upstairs flats, every set freshly hearthstoned in white, or cream
or blue; iron boot-scrapers carefully blackleaded; and brass
bell-pulls fairly shining, each a single eye looking on the
Sabbath calm. You went upstairs to a dim sitting-room in
which Grandma held state. Two sets of curtains, one of lace
starched to the thickness of perpendicular rice-pudding, the
other a weighty velveteen, allowed only a reverent sunshine
in. Even then it fell on nothing frivolous: a gilt and black
sarcophagus which was a Family Bible stood on a table by the
window; there was the huge prickly end of a horsehair sofa;
and surveying it in a particularly melancholy way were the
enlarged photographs of two dead young men, who would
have been my uncles if they had lived. It was an apartment
very suitable for receiving the Vicar in; and it truly repre-
sented Grandma's front on the wicked world.

But to understand it, you needed to go further in. You came
then to a living-room permanently untidied by the large
family that had grown up there. Its chief features were an
immense oval table, stained and ringed in many domestic
accidents and carelessnesses; and an ancient screen covered
with pictures all subdued by age to the authentic dinginess of

41

tint characteristic of an Old Master. The screen hid a scullery which was merely an enclosed landing on the stairs going down to the yard. A tap dripped and spluttered here into an old yellow sink, and from it came a strong smell of wet flannel and household soap which was there permanently like an atmosphere. That scullery opened on a different world—the one Grandma tried to turn her back on. Down below were the open middens and the swarming life of Oystershell Lane, a shocking slum.

Neither Sunday nor any day was sacred down there. It was never really quiet either. There was always a sort of simmer which now and then boiled over in a crescendo of battle-noises, filthy words, crashes of furniture flying through windows, shrieks and thuds, the wailing of the damned when a well-thrashed wife realized the full extent of the hurt to her and her home, and at last a long decrescendo of sobbing and low-voiced sympathy interrupted just at the end by a single anguished oath, shot into the night, and aimed perhaps at all creation. Creation, in Oystershell Lane, certainly deserved its epithet. It was very authentically four-lettered. Its joys were as adjectival as its woes, and when their choruses came quavering up from outside the boozer or a melodeon began squelching out tunes from a doorway to show a family was celebrating, the pacific stranger was well-advised to go another way. This was a human jungle. Every kind of life in it had raw edges, and was always coming into ear-splitting collisions which contracted the air around with an expectation of murder to be done, blue murder at that.

If the outbreak was very near, we children were shepherded away to the front of the house so that we should not hear it. This was Grandma's order. We stayed now subdued and safe in her rather awe-inspiring presence. She had fought through many long years to bring up her family against the danger that they might slip backwards into the Oystershell Lane horrors. The poverty they lived in made that fall always probable. Her husband's easy-going nature, his economic inconstancy, was no safeguard. Therefore she developed her own will, buttressed it strongly on the Bible and got sanction for it from the Church, until it was queenly and paramount, capable of bending all in that house towards the one certain succour of the Victorian poor, respectability. This was her whole technique of living. They might have no money to pay for schooling, nevertheless to school they must go, a good school where they would be thrashed and shamed for not paying. No matter, the respectable went to good schools. They might be warding off starvation with the barest and poorest fare, yet when the Vicar called there must always be cakes for his tea. Her children used to hang about the closed front room door, listening to the ecclesiastical hum within, and hoping the parson wouldn't eat all the cakes. He always did, though. Once my mother suggested, when told to go and buy these pastries, that the parson being a good man might make do on bread and butter. Grandma turned on her in savage fury—she was then a stout black-haired woman who would grind her teeth when in a rage—'You'd have us disgraced, would you? Have the Vicar thinking he's in that Lane there when he comes to my house? Go and do as you're told at once.'

She was white-haired when I knew her, getting old, but still orbed and sceptred with an authority which to her grandchildren was mixed with the supernatural. For instance, she expected us to be afraid of thunder. I wasn't. But when she explained that thunder was God's anger against the wicked, and the look in her eye suggested the likelihood of me being in that category, I yielded up my bravery and followed the others, sheepishly as they, into the back-bedroom where they always took refuge from possible thunderbolts. The smoky rainbow which sometimes bent among the city chimney-pots was God's promise to the faithful. Now when that appeared we were all bucked. We looked from the window to Grandma, knowing full well who the faithful was, and felt a bit proud of our connection with the heavens. Yes, but my father pooh-poohed all this. He said he'd watched rainbows out of his engine-cab all the way from Gateshead to South Shields, and they were all heathen in South Shields, anyway, Arabs that didn't believe in Jesus. As for thunderstorms, why did they have lightning conductors on churches? Couldn't they trust the Almighty's aim? Grandma would murmur darkly about the wicked in their pride, and though he stood there large and confident as ever I thought myself he was taking a risk. I thought I was when I repeated his arguments to my own cronies. Then there came a day when Grandma very nearly won the argument outright. With three of my cousins, I was crossing the Town Moor when a thunderstorm shaped itself in the sky behind us. We raced for shelter, but long before we could cover that wide expanse of open grazing, the rumblings and the lash of rain were on us. But our way went by one solitary tree. A man and a boy sheltered under it, and I wanted to. The eldest of the cousins overruled me, luckily, because when we had gone by some two hundred yards or so and were head down into the rain, the wet grass before us suddenly blanched with a brief electric brightness. There was a colossal crumbling crash straight after, and when we half-spun round in the momentary bewilderment of it, that tree was down, man and boy not to be seen. We heard afterwards that they

43

were both dead. Grandma read the little item out of the paper, and quite a number of speculative eyes turned on me since it was known that I had been in favour of joining that luckless or wicked pair. It shook me. It shook my mother. Father was not told about the occurrence: we felt it had been a very close shave and for the moment it was not advisable to make anything of our relationship to a large scoffer who might tempt another and more accurate fusillade.

These cousins of mine were always about Bath Lane Terrace, a number of them. Out of eighteen grandchildren, various selections and groupings were possible each Sunday. Each one at some time during the visit was exhibited to Grandma, talked to by various Aunties and teased by one or other of the humorous Uncles. We were then turned out into the street to play. That made room in the little house for the adults to have their tea. When they were fed, it was our turn. By then, my father was beginning to marshal the men for a walk to the pub, the women trying to look as disapproving as Grandma did and making remarks of a cautionary character. The uncles on their way out each contributed a copper or two for us to spend on sweets. So in another ten minutes the gathering was in three parts: men in the pub, children selecting farthings-worths of this and that at a little shop, and their mothers left to talk together and to resurrect something of their old feeling of being all one family. Of course, they talked a great deal about their husbands and children, especially the latter. They were always curious to know what Grandma thought. Had she noticed little Millie's quickness with a needle? Did she think Albert was as strong as he looked? Was she pleased when Sep won a watch for going five years never absent, never late at school? Grandma had no favourites—that was well-established. Quite impartially she gave to each of her visiting grandchildren, one sticky black bullet (a round mint sweet), before she brought her interview with the little sinner to a close.

No doubt she felt she had made a fair assessment of our characters, even if it was at variance with what the mothers thought. One day she surprised them all. With no warning of her intention, she called me to her and said she was giving me a present which I must treasure all my life. It was the Lord's Word she was giving me, a handsome and well-illustrated volume called the Prize Bible. What she said was what she always would say, and nothing unusual, but the grave sincerity of her tone made deeps behind the words and hinted that there were reasons why in our house this Word was needed and I should be the one to feel that need. She made me feel marked out and dedicated, and that she had seen through my

44

pretence that I wasn't. For that moment only, she and I were face to face, both knowing what we knew.

Mother, too, though she tried to be just naturally proud of the distinction come to her son, must have felt that it had reference to the unhappiness of life in Third Avenue and was not so very flattering to her, not all the way through. Her sisters were genuinely surprised. But this was nothing to the surprise they got when I actually read the thing, right through, cover to cover, as if it was *Chips* or *Hereward the Wake*. It was my father coming out in me, a real scoffer's trick; and, of course, it could do no good. They all looked upon the clever little horror with some distaste and askance—you have to imagine what it was like to be looked at askance by five aunties, some uncles, and a dozen cousins. Yet it was no stunt I was guilty of. I had no more intention of reading the Bible than any other boy in our street, or anybody else's, was likely to have. Here on a wet Saturday morning was this handsome volume, leather-bound, of clear bold type and frequent illustrations—I'd look at the pictures. They were gaudy and full of action, quite a lot of them. Look at the priests of Dagon with their blood-splashed knives; Jael creeping into the tent of Sisera; Egyptian chariots overwhelmed by the Red Sea; Judas gloating over his pieces of silver like a carroty-headed Quilp; the stars grouping themselves in the sky for St. John on his flat roof at Patmos. You simply had to read of these matters; and if the narrative didn't always come up to the quality of the illustrations, when it did, you had a story which stayed in your imagination and gave it something to glow with. I read on, session after session, past all the boring bits and finished it at last. That is all. I suppose it took some time to sink in because there were no immediate results of an untoward character, not even when I was made amply aware of my outrageous temerity. This was a pity in one way. For when the true quality of that unnatural meal did not begin to explode upon my inner life, Grandma was dead, beyond reproach or gratitude, whichever I would have chosen to offer her.

Father attended the funeral and gave her royal honours. For the last time, I believe, he put on his full wedding regalia of top hat, black morning-coat with tails, flowered waistcoat, striped trousers, spats and ebony walking-stick with an ivory handle. Moreover, he hired one of the new motor-taxis, and arrived in Bath Lane Terrace looking, he said, 'like the Duke of Bullfunkum'.

I forget whether we went with him. The fact that I forget indicates another deterioration in us considered as a family. About this time it was becoming rare for him to take us out on expeditions. 'Us' now included another little girl born some

three months after my seventh birthday. These two preg-
nancies and their issue kept mother fairly straight for the time
being and the beery Mrs. Buchan's influence in bounds, but
they sadly added to her troubles. She couldn't really cope with
us all. Despite the help of a curious dame called 'Fourpence',
who came in twice a week to clean up for that sum and her
tea, the house was usually very untidy, going to wrack and
ruin, my father said. Meals were becoming sketchy, except
when he was in attendance; washing-day was a heartbreak
which tended to be broken off earlier and earlier in favour
of a jug of beer; even baking-day, that high-point of the child's
week, was interrupted or curtailed so that the cooling of the
oven cut out the special supper of kidneys or sheep's heart
which the day erstwhile warranted. Mother was losing her
looks too. The slender, pretty lass of the ringlets, the quick
eyes and the dancing grace was becoming a pot-bellied slattern
of uneven spread, thrown out by her lameness so that she went
lumpy-do as she walked. Bad boys chanted after her 'Lumpy-
do, lumpy-do, peas and vinegar, peas and vinegar, lumpy-do.'
Older people gave her a too-audible sympathy, seeing her
struggle along with infant in push-chair and a toddler trailing,
or trying to get all aboard a tram.

Now my father hated that kind of comment with all the
sweeping, irrational hatred of a shy and self-conscious man
who had always successfully concealed this defect in a fine
appearance and loud confident speech. He could not come to
fair conclusion on this point. To him it was knives and
broken glass to walk out with a family which was such a sorry
spectacle in the streets that it attracted ridicule and pity. Pity!
Jesus, he couldn't stand that. It was worse than charity. Odd,
isn't it, that these graces of the well-to-do and happy so easily
and often gently bestowed should be such whips and acid to
the poor folk they are intended to benefit. Well, then, with-
out acknowledging any cowardice in this, father found excuses
to himself for limiting his public appearances with the com-
plete family.

He still took me about with him on occasion. We had a
more or less established practice on a mid-week night of the
dayshift of going to a new entertainment called 'the pictures',
or in older dialect, 'the pictors'. This was a cheap night out
for him. The pictures cost no more than a copper or two, and
my presence preserved him from extensive drinking if he
ran into any of his mates. He always did. The two of them
would disappear into a pub, leaving me outside. The mate
generally paused at the door to give me a penny on my
promising not to tell the wife (meaning mother) what they'd
been up to. Though this was done solemnly enough, and I

played up to it properly, of course it was all kid-ball: **father** didn't care a hoot who knew he'd been drinking. But I waited outside somewhat sunned by my inclusion in the masculine conspiracy against women. Outside? Yes, because of a new Act of Parliament the Liberals passed, no doubt on the best middle-class advice, which threw all children out of the public-houses and helped to make family wassail a secretive and suburban affair that the neighbours wouldn't know much about.

Because I was outside, my father had an excuse for the curtailing of good cheer which his economics as a raiser of young on a working-man's wage was asking for. Soon we made our way from pub to picture-hall to be followed all in good time, by many millions of born and unborn who were to find themselves propelled by the same reasons that moved us towards this organized dreaming in semi-darkness and drought.

It wasn't so very organized for us, of course. The hall was in fact, a shabby affair which must have been a mission at some time. It had no electric signs or elaborate foyers. There might have been a couple of posters, and there was an old woman sitting by the kerb selling little hard pears out of a soap-box on wheels. Inside, there was no ramp to the floor. The seating was forms or hard chairs linked in fives by planking. If you couldn't see at the back, you stood up; if the people in front of you stood up, you climbed on to your seat. This happened in moments of culminating excitement when on the screen—but it had ceased to be a screen; it was events we all saw with our own eyes—the faithful dog panted over the last ridge with the message that meant reprieve in its collar, or the blood of the wounded hussar dripped through the trap-door on to the table at which his enemies stood. I yelled and stamped on my seat, and was often in danger of falling into the next row or knocking somebody's hat off, all of which amused my father immensely. Most of the audience made some noise or other. You see, they were recruited from the music-hall and the melodrama; they had not yet learnt the separate and intro-verted enjoyment so proper to the Art of the Cinema. The fact that the pictures were silent gave everyone a natural right to comment as and when and how. They weren't taking the mike out of the show, by any means, no. Films were still far too real for anybody to be cynical about them. It was the utterly convincing reality of these scenes which compelled us to behave as though we were at the point of joining in upon them.

Half-way through there was a musical interlude during which patrons had time to withdraw for refreshment to the nearby boozer. The lights went up on a shallow stage behind a row of artificial flowers and ferns. At the side of that, a gramophone began playing. There was a great deal of shuffling in the rows as stout matrons in cloth caps and shawls and heavily moustached blokes in mufflers or celluloid dickies pushed their way out. Quite a lot of these worthies never returned. When that became apparent without doubt there would be a scramble for better seats on the part of those who reckoned themselves unsuited. But for the while we waited till the slides came on. The gramophone struck up 'When the Fields are White with Daisies, I'll Return', and the first slide showed on the screen as half the lights were dimmed. It showed a sailor taking leave of his sweetheart—upside-down because the operator had gone out for a drink, too, and his boy had taken over. As the gramophone scratched and hooted its way through the immortal ballad, we waited to cheer each new slide.

> When the fields are white with daisies,
>   And the roses bloom again—
> Let the love-light in your heart more
>   brightly burn.
> For I'll love you, sweetheart, always,
> So remember when you're lonely—
> When the fields are white with daisies,
>   I'll return.

At last, there was Jack with his kit-bag at the girl's feet and very truly the fields *were* white with daisies. We all joined in the final chorus and cheered its conclusion. Yes, but where was the operator? Very likely, after an interval of general unease and peering about, that last slide would wriggle across the screen and be held through a complete repeat of the song. The second half of the programme was often bulked out with films we had seen before, or with old news-reel material rather grossly re-edited in the projection box. A popular item such as King Edward's funeral got dished up in some very queer shapes as the continued ripping of sprocket-holes made more and more cuts necessary.

We were well-satisfied. I used to describe the whole show to my mother afterwards, and it always annoyed me that she couldn't be made to understand the magic of it. She thought it was some trick business, manifestly inferior to the theatre, that's why it was so cheap. She couldn't get it out of her head that it was mere hard-upness sent us there. Hard-upness, you see, was more than usually in the air then. The railwaymen were engaged in a series of strikes intended to raise their status to that of the skilled men in other branches of engineering. Were they skilled or not? Fitters, turners, millwrights all around us said they weren't; they hadn't served their time, and they couldn't make the locomotive engines they drove. My Uncle Will, a skilled man himself and destined very soon to wear the bowler hat or 'dut' of the foreman, used to make this point with all the reiterated dogmatism natural to a Sunderland man supporting a Sunderland thesis. Listening to him I felt he certainly had an argument though couched in curiously uncouth speech. (At that time, I was accustomed to hearing only the pure English spoken in Northumberland and on the Tyne and did not know that as you get deeper into Durham a tykey element creeps into the dialect as a sort of warning to the sensitive traveller that the bottomy dumps of Yorkshire are, indeed, imminent.) Yes, he'd got something, had blue-jawed Uncle Will. Was my father to be flattened? He wasn't. He delivered an attack on the other side of the board by affably remarking that if Will was right then the railway companies could sack their present staff in the next strike and replace them with unskilled men. Why didn't they do that? Because such chaps could not learn how to run trains in any short time. It takes longer to make an engine-driver or a fully qualified signalman than it does to make a fitter; and some of their skill is only to be got by long experience of the job. Many lives depend upon that skill; it must be acknowledged; it would be acknowledged when a few strikes had shown on what it was everybody was depending.

When I first heard these arguments, a strike seemed to me a pleasant matter, the adult version of a school holiday. Suddenly the incredible routine of work was broken in the middle of a week; father's work dickie and tie hung unregarded by the side of the grandfather clock; he dressed up in the morning to go to a meeting, returned full of beer and bonhomie to grace the dinner-table; after dinner, instead of pursuing the railwayman's invariable need of sleep, he took me into town. Here we kept on meeting mates of his. With each one there was a hold-up to discuss the situation, while I heeled the kerb or wondered at the way a dusty summer sky fretted with roof-tops got itself embalmed in the aspic of a plate-glass window behind us. These conversations were of little interest to me, of course. They were literally high over my head, up among the pipe-smoke, and so hard to follow even if I could understand their purport. But one of them took an unexpected turn. I heard the word 'treat'. This man, a fireman from Gateshead, wanted to treat us in some way, and father was putting him off. I craned up to hear better. The Gateshead fireman appealed to me, 'D'ye want to come to the theayter, laddie?'

49

Why, yes, I did, naturally. Father wasn't too pleased, and there was some more humming and hawing before it was agreed that we should meet our friend outside the Pavilion in time for first house.

Something must have gone wrong at the start of this evening—maybe they went for a drink and stayed too long—because we found ourselves having to stand at the back of the gallery, my father lifting me up to see. He couldn't offer to pay for a transfer to the pit seeing that it was the fireman's treat, so we had to stick it out rather too uncomfortably to enjoy the show. In fact, all I remember of it is the movement of the limes sweeping across the stage to follow the steps of some top-hatted tap-dancers, who were oddly foreshortened when seen from the height of the gallery and hopped about black in the mauve lights like birds—they were birds, too, Fred Karno's Mumming Birds, one of them a very rare bird indeed, when exhibited under a trickier kind of limelight, Charlie Chaplin.

It was much later before I realized that a strike was not only a jolly break in the work-routine, how much later there's no point in guessing since childhood's time is biological, its seasons move like eras and are counted among the creeping changes of the physical climate which successively cloud and crystallize in mannikin shapes about the young identity. It was Christmas, then, leave it at that. The shops had been decorated for long enough to get us all agog, their show of colours and tinsel sparkled behind the frost-rime on the windows, and it was, obviously, getting near the day when mother must make her annual expedition to buy the goose. This involved touching father for some extra money, always a hazardous and doubtful undertaking. He would yield in the end, but not easily; it was not his policy to let anyone get hold of an idea that he had money on tap, so to speak. Once we had the goose, Santa Claus and all the glory would surely follow. I still believed in Santa Claus, you see, although at the same time I knew quite well that the economics of Christmas depended upon my father's good will and the details of their administration upon my mother's journeys. I allotted to Santa the compartmented credence which my elders allow to God, or a patent medicine, or to what the stars foretell.

Well, I was in for a shock. My mother interrupted my Christmas anticipations with the news that we were on strike, we had no money (here was her empty purse as witness), and there'd be no Santa Claus. I was old enough to understand, she said, as the little girls weren't, and I must try not to show my disappointment. Later on, she'd make it up to us. This was flat, I knew: I walked out an older lad.

50

True, of course, had I noted it, there was curious stillness over the Avenues. Normally, at any hour of the twenty-four, if you looked along our street, you were bound to see at least one railwayman in work clothes, his bait-tin under his arm going to or from the junction. They were always about, hurrying along clean-faced towards the sharp dawn paling the signal lamps over the lines, drifting wearily back on an afternoon sun; in groups jolly and joking in the Chillingham Hotel or outside the social club, in pairs coming out of the light of the blue arc-lamps at the end of the shift and ready for their bed. Now that traffic was stopped. So was a lot of other kinds. The electric trains were silent in the cutting, the sudden blue rainbow they made ceased to flicker on the houses above; there were no puffs of steam or harsh mechanical panting behind the junction wall, no shunting noises like the slow collapse of huge iron playing cards against the buffers. I had seen that all this was happening, must have done, but it did not add up to mean anything until now. So on this frosty morning which began with the feeling of imminent festivity in the air, my mother's grave words were a sesame that walked me through a looking-glass into the real world beyond.

Chapter Seven

STREET-WARFARE

The strike was over by New Year. Railway strikes never lasted long because they hit a wide public immediately and caused such a maximum discomfort all manner of interests shouted for a settlement. We did not have to endure the long drawn-out misery of the miners' battles. Also, we generally won. In this one, there had been no great hardship. The Christmas dinner was rabbit with mashed swede turnip, divided in the order of one hind leg to father, one to me; one fore leg to sister, one to mother; bits for the baby, and kidneys to whoever father fancied at the moment—perhaps himself. Afterwards we had no toys to take out into the street and swank around, but there was a fire in the front room and some oranges, attenuated good cheer. The drought-stricken head of the family filled in his hours by giving all the clocks in the house a clean-up, spreading newspapers on the table and polishing away at brass pointers or tickling fine oil into the various works. His wife, even more savagely drought-stricken probably, shifted the baby from her bad leg to the good one and tried to read her book against its whimpering. Altogether, it was a very quiet do.

At New Year the strange paralysis on the world of work lifted. A trickle of coin began to drip into the housewives' purses. In our house we even had belated Christmas presents. I got a small train set, which mother was over the moon about because it had been marked down to 1s. $0^1{}_2$d. as a result of having missed its proper period of sale before the holidays. I didn't share her enthusiasm for a bargain. It was a poor thing, born out of season, my imagination wouldn't warm to it. The little engine couldn't hold to its circle of light uneven rails; it hadn't enough spring power to cross the floor—hell with it!

But the real engines down the junction were running again, and presently I had one of them to play with. This was the result of one of the utterly unexpected tremendous gestures my father used to make just once in a way. He was running a shunting engine at this time, and often coming from school, I would hang around the big gate of the yard with some of my pals proudly pointing out his operations to them. He must have seen me, but instead of putting an instant embargo on the practice, which must have been his first idea, I bet, one evening he stepped down from the engine-cab and strolled towards me, calling me to come to him. I hung back, naturally; my pals got ready to run. Several times he called. I answered only with an uneasy, 'What?' At last I thought it safest to take a few steps towards him. He reached forward, picked me up, and said easily, 'Come on, I'll give you a ride.'

I hardly dared believe that he could actually mean I was to ride on an authentic locomotive, but a glance back at my two little pals standing so quiet and awed, forlorn at being left out of such a miraculous treat, certainly indicated that it really was going to happen. It did, too. Almost stupefied with the wondrous rarity of the event, I found myself climbing up steep, metal steps, hauled in by father's mate, and here I was close to the great steam pulse, passing by the fire-box and hoisted on to the driver's seat with the caution to keep my head in whenever an inspector came by. You see, the whole thing was illegal: that was another knock-out. You couldn't imagine suchaoneas my father breaking railway rules. Not that I feared for him, mind you (I took the inspector story as largely kid-ball) but it was so unlikely that he'd make this vast enlargement of the very fabric of life merely for the sake of amusing me.

Well, it was a terrific evening. All were agreed, whether it was the driver, the fireman or one of the shunters hopping on to the engine step, that now I was on the railway I must earn my keep. The fireman, pretending to be tired, handed me his shovel—I struggled to get a lump or two clear of the fire-box door into the fanning heat of caked flame behind; the driver instructed me how to pull the whistle chain when he gave the word—I got some strangulated blasts out of it which I could only hope the signalmen and shunters knew how to interpret; and all our visitors were insistent that I should keep my eye continually on the gauges, that was most important— I watched the water-level fluctuating in the glass-tube and duly reported any major change. While I was so busy, the little side-tanker was usually trundling along, banging into a row of trucks, or reversing and trailing one of them with a great rattle over a series of points, for the complicated operations of shunting were in full progress. My head was often bumped against the side of the cab, but I was so occupied in trying to follow all the moves made and the many instructions I was given to watch this and look out for that, I noticed no minor discomforts. Nor even the flight of time. Presently, we ran out on a far line near the big gate and stopped. The engine settled down to a regular sighing; the fireman got out a clean bucket and started washing his hands.

Looking out, at a quite unfamiliar view of the houses on Chillingham Road, it surprised me to see they were in such a sudden darkness and that a young moon, bright as a razor, was ready to drop among their chimney-pots. The pub lights came on as I looked. Obviously my day of glory must come to an end soon.

When I squirmed back towards the inside of the cab, I was handed a bottle of warmed-up tea to drink, then a sandwich from my father's bait-tin which tasted strongly of the tin, or of railways, or of both. The mate produced an apple. And this was the end. After all concerned had done a lot of elaborate peering around to see that we were not overlooked by any boss's men, my father got down on to the ground and I followed. He watched me as far as the gate, then I ran home boiling like a pot full of dumplings with the richness of my experiences.

For near a week, I was a big-shot on the corner. Even the bigger lads were prepared to listen to my account of an experience so unusual, so much to be envied. At least they were until I began ornamenting the tale, bit by bit, in fact to such an extent that it seemed in the end somewhat unreal to me when I came to think of it. I dropped it as a matter for public consumption, though when only Wilf and Freddie (the two boys who witnessed my ascension) were about, it came alive again since they felt they'd so nearly shared in the exploit, you could practically call it theirs.

Then a bigger matter blew up one evening. I was on Daddy Hilton's corner, hanging about hoping to get into a game of Kick-the-Block, when sounds of battle drifted down from the Fourth Avenue entrance. Sticks and stones were flying; war-cries chanted. From nowhere the words 'Chapman Street gang' got uttered on the anonymous air. Chapman Street, now, ran from Chillingham Road, but on the other side of the railway bridge, down to Parson's Works. The lads from its corners and those of the streets next to it had a long-standing feud with our lot in the Avenues. At long intervals, it would boil over into a regular battle. Then they invaded us, or we invaded them; the signal that such an attempt was on being the appearance of large bodies in battle array on the bridge. Their numbers, you see, indicated that several corner-gangs had joined forces, and, therefore, all smaller wars were subordinated to the main regional rivalry. Often enough the invaders were met and turned back on the bridge itself; this time, however, we were caught napping. The invaders seemed to be already overwhelming the weak Fourth Avenue forces. They would soon be in command of the bend going in to Third back lane, which was a strategic point of high

54

value to us since it allowed us a choice of changing over in mid-battle to an attack on the rear of any force which advanced beyond that entry without first capturing it. Too late to get up there, though. We'd be lucky to halt the Chapman mob at Fifth.

Our corner and Sixth rushed off to get hold of weapons. The five Robson brothers could be trusted to hold their own Fifth for a bit. Meanwhile Wilf and I, being young, but not absurdly so, must race off to arouse Seventh and Eighth, if we could.

By luck, we found the surly Seventh in just the right mood. They were all assembled on one corner and talking together gloomily. They'd just had the police after them over a matter of a large parcel of cigarettes knocked off that very afternoon from their own corner shop at the bottom of their street. And none of them had done it! They didn't know who had. So the air about Seventh was knit up with rankling injustice, heavy with frustrated vengeance, and melancholy because of the mirage of smokes they might have had if they hadn't been so uselessly honest. Now Wilf and I were rather in the position of a couple of Cherokees appearing unarmed before the war-painted Choctaw tribe. We had to rattle off our message before we were scragged—we did all of that twice over. It was just the news to suit present moods round these parts: Seventh started up as one man—yes, they'd be in any trouble that was going.

Wilf and I ran on to Eighth. But there was nobody on their corners, as far as we could see. A little way down the street, their girls were skipping with a big rope, two turning, the rest running in, pair after pair, while all chanted, 'Never mind the weather, girls; in and out the fire, girls.' We asked the girls who were waiting where the lads were. They at once rushed on us, grabbed our caps and chucked them into the gardens. 'Had away to your own street,' they yelled.

We climbed over to get our caps, jumped the next garden railings, and the next, thus by-passing the big skipping game and getting down towards the bottom of the street. In one doorway sat wee Alfie Bell, his leg in plaster and a pile of comics by him. He told us. 'They're all down at the Chink's —that's where they are. What d'ye want them for?' He wanted to keep us talking, but we only yelled the news over our shoulders as we pelted on, 'Big fight on in Third—Chapman Street out.'

At the bottom we almost collided with the Eighth Avenue lot who were scattering away before the charge of an infuriated Chinaman brandishing a knife—at least, that's how they would have described it. Really, old Fong Lee was never infuriated and didn't carry a knife. There, he was shuffling back towards the laundry now, his blue shirt tail flapping on his thin behind. He turned at the door to shake a skinny fist, grinned at a couple of passing railwaymen, and popped inside. Yet he had plenty reason to be annoyed. Oriental patience might withstand the loud chanting of 'Ching, Ching, Chinaman, choppy, choppy, chop,' by a choir of tone-deaf twerps around his door, but when that door was frequently flung open, its bell jangling, to enable one of that choir to fling in a couple of damp horse-turds that might land among the parcels of finished washing, then the love of cleanliness natural to a laundryman must have been offended beyond the immediate consolation of Chinese philosophy.

But Wilf and I had to get the attention of some of these hopping, taunting boys at once. When we did they all gathered around and lay on each other's necks listening to us. Being still excited they didn't jump to arms, but after some rather idle questions they thought they had better be in on this in case they were accused of cowardice later.

We were agog to be back ourselves, but we waited, thinking to make a more effective return if accompanied by the reinforcements that were bound to give us victory.

Our hasty plan was to come on the scene via Sixth, creeping along the gardens or stealing from path to path so that we shouldn't be noticed, a flank attack or reinforcements according to how far the battle had swayed. It was obvious at first sight that the home forces still held the entry to Sixth, though the fighting extended beyond there. This fighting, of course, was never serious in the adult sense of the word. The warriors carried wooden swords or just lengths of wood, cardboard shields, cane bows with tar-tipped arrows, lengths of string weighted at the end to be used alternately as bull-roarers and bolos, and they picked up small stones or any handy road-filth as they went along. There was plenty of noise and banging of stick against stick, sudden rushes and hand-to-hand struggles as weapons were lost or abandoned, but no one was ever hurt beyond a general bruising and scratching. Police intervention was never necessary, though it could happen if a copper just occurred along that way. The battles came to an end usually when a sufficient number of adults round about had realized the unusual scale of the tumult and began to gather for its suppression.

That is how this one finished. Chapman Street army could get no further now that the forces engaged were more nearly equal, and were beginning to retreat. They would have to, in any case, because Third Avenue parents were now at their doors and a lot of our lads were being ordered to lay down their arms. It was recognized as not fair to keep on engaging an enemy who had half the fight knocked out of him by having to listen to mother's shouts while in the act of laying on. There was Mrs. Robson for a start. The Robsons still held the stable at the end of their back lane but the appearance of this fury from the soap-suds who stood with arms akimbo like a village blacksmith who'd grown a bust, would quell them in a matter of seconds. She was a She-who-must-be-obeyed, she was, and well the Robsons knew it. The barber was out, too. Waving his razor, he, and clearing his fore-court of all the misbegotten swarming of unadulterated boy like magic. The mad woman at No. 52 was dancing in her garden—with rage; it had been trampled. We left her plenty of room. She was liable to run out at Boy, and nip it. Other women, including Wilf's mother and mine, were merely vocal. They *could* fetch their men, mind, but not readily because it wasn't policy for them either to draw uncertain-tempered males into it—oh, lord, there was old Braden, red-faced and in his socks. If he had to put his boots on, IF-F-F—— The word whistled among us like steam from his locomotive when it had too much head on, and we who knew all about his terrible corns could imagine, nearly, the retribution that would come to us. The fight went out. It was exeunt omnes, or 'all had away by yourselves'.

Chapman Street had won, no blinking this fact. We could deny their claim to have held all Third Avenue (they never did), and argue it was only half (it was rather more) but there couldn't be much heart for us in the discussion. Better to dream of revenge; better again to plan it.

Now a group of the younger ones, including myself, had just acquired a marvellous headquarters. One of our recent recruits had a father who was manager of the Working Men's Club. It occupied commodious premises, as the bills say, in an old house standing in its own grounds half-down the slope that ended at the Chillingham Hotel. The commodiousness aforesaid included stables and a large gravelly yard about them which was a dump for barrels and crates of empties. For small boys there were negotiable paths winding into the middle of the barrel fleet, and a space here which could be roofed over with loose planks so as to make a place of secret and unlawful assembly just large enough for four or five of us. New chum, Stan, our host, could be trusted to knock off a packet of Gold Flake; we collected the best of the empties from the crates of Gamle-Carlsberg (lager because there was naturally more left in the bottoms); and here we could sit drinking and smoking as much at our ease as were our fathers in the bar next door. The Act of 1910 shut the pubs on us infants—right, now we were secret drinkers, the natural or illegitimate product of prohibition.

Here we often dwelt on immense plans for the complete subjugation of Chapman Street. Somehow the thing smouldered in our imaginations: every now and then we fairly lit ourselves up in the mutual contemplation of projected enterprises at the very least as colourful and glorious as the famous storming of Front do Boeuf's castle. No doubt the drainings of flat lager helped, also the smoke from the genuine Virginian tobacco which layered the beer-scented air between the barrels, wavered and curled in blue-grey gossamer scarves like a genie about to take shape. The plans came to no immediate fruition. *We* had not yet the authority of sufficient years to give us leadership and as it happened a whole crop of our bigger lads were just then arriving together at the age when they must put away childish things. For a time, there was none ready to take their place. An eon or two must have passed before there came along an evening when our long-forgotten projects suddenly resurrected themselves. Under our leadership, the united Avenues swept over the bridge. The result, though not the panoply or the derring-do, completely realized our dreams. We forced a passage through the stinking back-lanes of the Chapman Street area (it had no flush-lavatories, and the weekly collection by cart seemed always over-due); captured all the main corners; broke up a last stand by Parson's works; and for a wonderful quarter of an hour could parade unchallenged all over the enemy territory. After that, I laid down my tin shield (which started life as a blazer for the kitchen fire), put up my trusty quarter-staff (but not back on the oak picture-frame it came from)— the age of chivalry and knightly jousting was ended.

We'd lost our haunt among the barrels before this. Stan's father got the sack, which meant that they had to move; the new manager had no children, nor any tolerance of boys; so we were teetotallers again and back on the corner. There the slow-moving seasons brought each their distinctive sports and appropriate pestering of neighbours. Every one of these came in with the unannounced unanimity of an unconscious communal instinct. One particular winter's morn, for instance, every mother's boy of us would begin rummaging in drawers trying to find old keys with hollow ends. What on earth for? You might well ask if you were a parent. Go outside and you'd see. The key was tied to a piece of string attached at the other end to a nail; the hollow end of the key was filled with a mixture of potash and sulphur, the nail rammed into it; and thus loaded it was swung hard against a wall. There was an explosion. A sulphur stain flared on the wall. Every corner resounded with small bangs, and after a week or two, there was scarcely one hard projecting surface about that wasn't yellowed with many sulphur bursts. Then, suddenly as it first happened, it was over.

Now young Willie and Albert were spreading a different disorder in their homes. There was an unholy reek of spilt paraffin, hanging round the domicile. It appears this time that most of the boys have somehow acquired bull's-eye lanterns of the accredited police pattern. The black winter streets hear the cry of 'Jack, show a leet.' You are perhaps just about to trip over a small body lying in cover by your garden railings, except that at that cry the body flashes a beam of light into the street, switches off again and scrambles away to another hide. Behind him he leaves a smell of burning paraffin and hot blistering paint. In seconds another boy arrives running, his lantern openly shining. He rakes both gardens with it, swings it to the opposite side of the avenue, sees no one, and bawls again, 'Jack, show a leet!' Now and then the distance may be lit up with a real flare: somebody has tripped or dropped his lantern and the oil pouring out of the container has lighted all at once.

There was quite a lot, one way and another, adults had to be wary of during the dark evenings. You may be walking out for your supper beer and suddenly you see just on the rim of the lamp-light that someone has dropped a nice fat purse. Honest or dishonest, whichever you be, you stoop to pick it up—it travels away from you just before your hand can close on it. But if it is not a purse, only a parcel obviously dropped from an over-filled shopping bag, *that* won't travel; it can be picked up easily—not that its contents will do anybody any good. It pays to think twice. Even in a simple matter like going into a shop—look twice at the door-handle. It is possible that the lads have been down the lanes lifting the wooden flaps in the walls that hide the shit-buckets so that they can dip in their sticks, and have daubed the handles of several local shops with a mixture which is going to do your gloves no good if you touch it.

Such pesterings were planned beforehand on the corner, and so were what the courts would call our petty thefts. A crowded shop was to us a fine opportunity of mingling in and knocking off apples or eggs or anything that was near enough to our pockets to be quickly pouched. But shops were not always crowded. At some of them, anyway, we were too well known to escape the eagle eye. If one of us had a coin to spend, though, the procedure was simple. We picked something for him to buy, which was right down in the very front of the window. All accompanied him inside and when fat Mrs. Wilson or rheumaticky old Bennett was struggling to reach along the window display, we rapidly filled our pockets with anything in reach. No shop-keeper dared leave any empty bottles, on which there was a charge, anywhere that we could get at. I've known us go into the newsagents to look at the comics, or buy Dad's paper, and come out with a couple of lemonade bottles the confederates had concealed. Once we had a real windfall in this line. A newcomer to the off-licence was careless enough to stack his empties in a shed down his yard which was latched but not locked. One of our spies reported this at once, and for some days we were millionaires almost. However, hard times set in pretty regularly. We got rumbled too much. Then all that was open to us in this boy-cautious neighbourhood, was the capture of a few potatoes or dog-biscuits, the only edible goods any of our shopkeepers would display near enough to the door to be handy for us.

Far more often, of course, we were fully occupied with the many games that made their immutable processions across our year. Marbles, tops, hoops and girds, bays, monty-kitty, kick-the-block, up-for-Monday, they came and went in their due seasons. My chief pal for some of these years, Wilf Rowley, often returned with me into the more private play of fantasy. His father was a joiner. He built a shed in their back-yard and put up a flag-post against it. This contraption very soon became a line-of-battle ship, having logs of wood mounted as cannon, in which Admirals Nelson and Collingwood sailed off to meet the French. (I was Collingwood, probably because he was a favourite of my father's being a Tynesider who lived up to his quality when he pointed out that Nelson's famous signal on the day of Trafalgar, when he spelled it out, was a fuss about nowt, or words to that effect.)

One night as it was getting dusk we were still pacing our quarter-deck when Wilf's mother opened the scullery door, as I thought, to call him in. I was used to this melancholy happening. Most nights one after another of my pals would be called away from me, till I was left alone. Me, I never wanted to go home, because I never knew what misery or quarrelling I'd find there. So I was prepared to slink back to the corner-end to while away some more evening somehow. But tonight Mrs. Rowley surprised us both by asking me to supper. Old Wilf was delighted; he thought his mother had turned up trumps very unexpected, and that this concession must be in honour of Easter, this being the Saturday of that festival. I should have been delighted too, more so than he, but I thought I detected something odd in her manner. Still, and all the same, we sat down to a somewhat cissy meal of cocoa and biscuits. Then she remarked brightly, that since it was Easter, I could stay the night—wouldn't that be nice? At once a fear

60

for my family clutched me; I choked on my cocoa (which in any case and by its own right is a pretty glottis-curdling kind of drink to give to a poor child).

There was something very bad at the back of this kindness —something to do with my mother, I guessed. But a sort of shame kept me from asking what it was; I didn't know otherwise how to put off the invitation; and there was Wilfy pleased as punch. I don't think I made any reply. But presently, I hid my apprehensions under a whirl of chatter which never ceased until we were about to go to bed. Here, by the bed, Wilf got down on his knees—what, to pray? I could have stood that from my colleague the ex-Lord Nelson, but he wasn't; he was actually kneeling to pee in the pot. What's more, his mother standing behind us expected me to do the same. I went to lift it up—oh, no, mustn't, both told me, kneel down so as you don't drop it or spill it. Why damn it, I knew how to piss in a pot properly. Hadn't I seen my father many a night standing in his shirt with his back to mother and me, holding the pot in one stout thumb and patiently filling it to the brim. That was the way. I complied with this Roman habit, but I can't say that I enjoyed the result.

No sooner were we in bed than we heard a knock on the front door. Wilf wanted to go on talking, but I kicked him and listened painfully. It was my father come to collect me. We were in the back bedroom, and I couldn't make out what was said. But it was something that had happened to mother. I was very frighteningly sure of that—what? An ultimate disaster, or nothing much—what? The slow, happy Wilfred was at last alive to matters; he asked what was up. I told him 'nothing' very sharp. That completely shut him up, and it wasn't long before his slower easy breathing indicated that he was asleep. For me an uneasy night stood over this alien bed; its questions kept me pricked and tense for what seemed a long time before the oblivion due to the hour and my years finally swept upon me.

Chapter Eight

THE DISMANTLING OF A CRUCIFIX

Easter morn broke fine and bonny, its early sunshine so very
delicate and new it splashed upon the unfamiliar wallpaper
of this bedroom as though reflected from a sheet of water. But
as soon as I was awake I wanted to be gone. My fears were
not so pressing by daylight, but my curiosity was. Let me but
know, I felt, and then my world will re-establish itself some-
how, but I must know first. My hosts either didn't guess that,
or were so taken up with hospitality and the emotions appro-
priate to the season they couldn't spare me a single delaying
kindness. Wilf's Da was about now (don't know where he'd
been the previous night), and so was his young sister. Neither
were in the habit of saying much when I was present. The
sister fastened her large blue eyes on me and kept them there
until I felt I was wearing them, like a pair of coloured spec-
tacles; her father never looked directly at me at all, but he
made a series of very poor jokes intended to make me feel at
home—he made them in the air, the way a man might snap
his fingers. At each one, baby sister inclined a ringlet without
lowering her gaze; for the more successful Wilf giggled into
me, and I had to giggle back into him.

We were eating Easter eggs while this went on. First, the
fruit of the hen, but dyed for the occasion blue, yellow, red
and coffee-colour, then when we were expected to be reason-
ably full up Mrs. Rowley produced some chocolate eggs which
Wilf didn't know she had. Oh, he was pleased with her all
right. He kept glancing to see that I was. I should have been,
yes, but then I should have been enjoying this exceptional
breakfast, and I wasn't. I ate as if I was being paid piece rates
for the job, efficiently, but not putting any soul into it. Besides,
Mrs. Rowley would come to rest every now and then half-way
through the kitchen door and bend a speculative eye on me
as if she was trying to recollect what was wrong with the boy.
Maybe she was a natural spyer-out of human nudity—at any
rate there came prominently in my mind during that break-
fast an example of her talent for witnessing that up till then
I hadn't thought of. It was this: one night during the
previous summer when there was something of a heat-wave
on, my father came home late after a long shift so sweat-staled

62

and coal-dusted he thought he'd have a bath. Our house, of course, had no bathroom. What he used, as and when convenient and worth all the bother, was a thing called the poss-tub, a sawn-off port-wine barrel regularly used on washing-day for possing clothes in. It stood in the yard under the scullery window unless anybody lugged it indoors. This late night, being silken and summery with a low lapsing moonshine as warm as milk and the houses about blind in sleep, father put himself to no more trouble than to fill the tub. He chucked off his weighty work-clothes and climbed into the tub, secure of solitude, he thought, and fearing no chill. Presently, though; presently, he felt eyes upon him. From where? His sensation directed his own gaze to the next upstairs scullery window. And there by the slight fold of a lifted curtain, he encountered an Eye. Now I appreciated this story because I, too, was encountering that Eye, frequently. It was Mrs. Rowley's, and there was no doubt about it, the woman was a natural overlooker.

Now you'd think when that breakfast at last came to an end I'd rush off home. But I didn't. Most of me wanted to still but the old reluctance to take up my unhappy family heritage came to tether me. I hung around until Mr. Rowley began blacking his and Wilf's boots in preparation for some Easter visiting upon relatives. At that, abruptly, I went.

Whoever lived in our house got so clairvoyant they could read the prevailing atmosphere before they were half-way down the passage. Today, as most days, the front door stood open; I turned the handle of the glass-door and before I'd quite reached the old coats hanging forever undisturbed on their hooks, my weather report was made out; clear, cool, after the storm. Add also that my father had gone to work, for I knew that too almost instantly. In the kitchen, mother was moving about rather efficiently; she looked excessively clean and drastically sober. My little sisters were sitting on the mat, playing with a couple of wooden Easter eggs which unscrewed and contained each a horrible dangling thing supposed to represent a serpent—just the sort of contraption little girls love and which adults always imagine are more suitable for boys. There was a bigger egg of a different kind for me, probably something with a ribbon, which boys always love. But I don't remember it, and I wasn't interested just then—I wanted to know.

My mother didn't want to tell me, and wouldn't for a while. Then I suppose she realized I was bound to hear from other sources, so she gave me the bitter barebones of the story. Because she had to tell me like this, out of my right to hear, and not for any pleasure she could have in telling, I felt the gravity of more years than I had to my name buttressing my attention. This was what happened. Yesterday afternoon, on her shopping rounds, she stopped at the Addison for a glass of beer, leaving the pram outside. She only had a couple, but when she came out and was pushing the pram containing younger sister and holding on to the hand of the elder, she had to pass a young policeman. She could feel him staring at her (many people did that, alas!). The awful thought came into her mind that he had seen her coming out of the pub and might think she was drunk (because she walked so badly and her hat and her hair were always being shaken loose by her uneven gait). At that moment, her lame foot caught on the sweeping hem of her skirt, the pram-handle went down under her weight, the baby yelled from fright. Over comes the copper to help. Yes, but he did think she was drunk. He wanted to run her in; worse, he did run her in; kids, pram as well, all the way to Headlam Street Police Station.

God, I could see it so vividly, that shame-making procession, the flushed, protesting, limping woman still hanging on to one whimpering child; the smart young copper holding her free arm and trying to steer a pram-full of yelling babe past curious and unsympathetic bystanders. It was such an unlikely parade it should never have been allowed to turn out. No Fate, not the most malicious, should have the power to display an unhappy family so publicly. That's what my mother thought, enraged as she was at the indecency of this comic Calvary she was so suddenly and unkindly cast for.

The cell, or wherever she was put, could have been only a short relief. Of course, she realized there was little chance of clearing herself at the police station. She was by now in such a state that even the charitable would rather assume that a cheerful old enemy, Drink, was the cause, rather than know they were witnessing the accidental breaking-point of many tensions. It was quiet in here, true, the fantastic spectacle was over, but that allowed her to contemplate more completely the terrible certainty that her husband would have to know about this. She feared his wrath more than anything the law might do. After all, she loved him; the law is just what one abides. But she dared not even hope that he would see this for what it was, a cruel mischance overtaking a woman who was not drunk, but lame, tired and fatally flustered.

It was some hours before they found my father. Rumour had been all round the Avenues before that and put me to an untimely bed, thus adding another exasperating circumstance to mother's bill for the day. Somebody now had to come and bail her out. And that somebody, I bet, must have gone up to the police station in a grand fury, planning to collect the

64

children and present the police with one drunken wife to have and to hold forever, permanently. There was no drunken wife on the premises, though. Either her long ordeal had sobered her up or, what I think more likely, she had never been drunk. Anyone who has ever had close dealings with women must have been struck by the curious knack they have of being impossibly in the right, and genuinely so, just at that point when you think you really have got them. They get murdered for this, frequently, but it still is so. Yes, I believe she was not drunk, and had never been. But undoubtedly, at the start of all this, she'd look it.

Her husband gave her a thrashing and forced her to sign the pledge. 'Forced her' was a phrase she used later to excuse her breaking it. As I saw her that queer calm Easter Sunday morning she'd have willingly signed anything that proclaimed or aided the strict virtue she was now wedded to.

I cannot remember making any comment when I had heard the end of this stripped narrative. But its effect on me was powerful. I went over lock, stock and barrel to my mother's side of the argument; I held that whatever she did was forgivable, and that what my father and the police did was not; I cared for her, without approving or admiring, and hell with all the moralities made by fortunate conformers by which they condemned and did not assist her. If she was to be outcast—and I was sure she'd continue to be—then I would be outcast too. For a start, I'd secretly drop my name of Kiddar and become William Johnson, adopting her maiden name as my standard.

At once the world of outer circumstances gave its chime to this decision. Forgotten in yesterday's upheavals there lay in the pram bottom a second-hand book mother had bought for me because it was only a penny and you never knew what I might read next. It was a slim volume meant for the use of schools containing some extracts from Boswell's *Life of Johnson*. Johnson! The very name I'd just put on as symbol of my dedication and a name of very great power indeed according to this book. I read it and re-read it, for Lord knows it was a terribly attenuated version of the huge Boswellian opus; you had to read it many times before the figure of the great Doctor inflated itself to somewhere near the true magnitude. When that happened, he became my hero, this Johnson of Johnsons.

Well that was fine, I had my exemplar, now for the discipleship. This proved curiously difficult. The matter bothered me quite a lot whenever I reflected on it. Something was expected of me, or at least I expected something of myself. But what? Where could I lay hold of the mantle of the master and make good my claim to be of his sect? I was fond of argument, for instance; I took delight in my father's encounters with insurance men and others calling at our house; I'd listen keenly and follow the logical manoeuvres. But any attempt I made to join in was discouraged or dismissed. Besides it wasn't easy to be ready with a crushing Johnsonian rejoinder at the right moment when you hadn't the physique for delivering it. I turned the pages dealing with the great man's schooldays to see if there was any help there. No, hardly a bit. Such a very different school his. For us scholarship was not a thing you wore as an elegant and perhaps an astonishing accomplishment, it was something you won. At our school we had no Latin and even less Greek. The only subject remotely resembling these was a weekly ordeal called 'English Composition'. With some doubt that it was a daft thing to do I began to introduce a little of the Johnsonian touch into these ragged little essays. 'Mother Nature's Spring-cleaning' this year had some new features in the laborious catalogue we always put down for that subject, it was the 'tintinnabulation of rain' which helped the growth of 'verdant foliage' now. Made the teacher sit up a bit, I bet!

In general, though, the world of Doctor Johnson was so unknown to me, I couldn't really see what he was trying to do. He wrote a dictionary—yes, well, you'd only to look at a dictionary to appreciate that that was an heroic job all right. He knew all the words, give him that. And he always won his arguments. But what were they about? Why were they so important to all these gladiators of the verbal arena? Our history lessons, you see, had nowhere near reached the eighteenth century. We were still bogged among the Plantagenets, and by the same method of slow torture employed in the issue of books for class-reading, it was all too likely that next term would find us starting the Plantagenets all over again. In fact it might easily take us as long to get down the centuries as it did the folks who originally made the trip, except that in one class or another we were bound to encounter a teacher who dropped us quickly down a ladder of dates into an era he had been reading up on.

My own reading was no help either in this case. I held a ticket for a public library but in the juvenile section. You were not allowed to browse or handle books before drawing them out. The procedure was to look over titles and authors in a catalogue, find the numbers, and then check on an indicator board to see if the books you wanted were out or in. Not very good, you know. Necessary because open access would have been a temptation to us to go knocking-off in the hope of raising a copper from the second-hand shop—to us an ill-gotten penny was sudden wealth—but not ideal. The system tended to canalize our curiosity about books into a safe and time-saving pursuit of a few popular authors: the whole of Henty was ever before us.

At home there was no such thing as a library, of course. But the lavatory sometimes blossomed with literature of a curious diversity. Lavatory is another of those stupid words—water-closet, we called it, using the exact Elizabethan term. It lived down the yard, being one-half of a brick-and-tile structure which also contained the coal-house; and we went out to it, necessarily, in all weathers. This is easily the best arrangement for such matters. Indoors, especially if it is lavatory and bathroom combined in the unholy tautology of house-agents, you get a somewhat squalid commingling on the score of comfort. A man should be private in his privy. He should never sit like a spider, his senses continually alerted to the plucked web of family noises and being reminded by them of actions and emotions not at all consonant with the job in hand, if one can call it that. He should be passive, too. Even if driven by a brutal urgency in the first place, passivity is his after-pleasure; and its spell is more readily put on if the outer world and its weather comes close by the door. Our water-closet possessed these qualities. In winter it was warmed against frost by a small oil lamp so that as you paused at the scullery door before taking off in a hen's scatter through rain or snow across the cement yard, you saw the fingers of weak yellow light feeling out through the chinks of door and tile, getting well-splashed with a rain far more continuous where there was light or touching and spinning the great dilatory snowflakes. Sometimes I teased myself with the thought that perhaps somebody was sitting there already, a stranger on our throne. No time to bother, though. Swing open the door on a patent emptiness, and catch it back quickly against the night—you're in.

Probably it was damned cold. Not that the walls were white-tiled in that fashion which gives to the public lavatory the suggestion of a hygienic lunatic asylum where you are temporarily locked up; no, these were plaster walls painted a mild red (all utility surfaces in our place tended to come to that colour in the end because red paint was the easiest sort to acquire for anybody working on the railway), and on the walls were nailed no less than three engravings of paintings by Marcus Stone. The throne itself was a rectangle of scrubbed board. It was solid and spacious, not like those silly hoops of petrified horse-collar which are always bobbing up and down or clinging to their patrons' buttocks at the moment of rising. There was room here, so there was room for books.

Don't get an idea that the books were there, primarily, as reading matter. Not so. In those days either the toilet roll had not been invented or else it was simply that all worthy folk would have thought it quite mad to spend money on mere bumf, anyway every one of these convenient outhouses or messuages which dotted our district held a supply of printed paper. You could learn something of the character of the household by studying it. For instance, we nearly always had a supply of railway time tables—not those issued to the public but the weighty volumes given to engine drivers so as to keep them up to date with alterations to running times, stops at certain stations and changes in the arrangement of signals. Many a sunny fly-haunted afternoon I've sat kicking my heels to keep away pins and needles from my dangling legs as I turned these pages. They were interleaved at places with buff or pink pages which gave one the idea that these were last-minute interventions of some dramatic quality. If so, what it was defied lay perusal. They held the same time-tables asterisked so that you could see below for working instructions, the same small illustrations showing signal arms of various types. I thought at one time of making a code out of these latter, but they were on the dull side and a bit obvious as anything numerical is in the way of cypher messages. The reading matter was dull too. Generally a couple of footnotes was enough to send me back to the list of stations: Scotswood, Wylam, Prudhoe, Stocksfield, Riding Mill, Corbridge, Hexham, Wall, Chollerford, Wark, Falstone, Plashetts, Redesdale, Bellingham, Deadwater and away over the Border. There was the Tyne leaving industry behind as it went up by the Roman Wall and the ruined camps, past half a dozen castles and out to the wide moors of the old debateable land. Or the coastal track: Amble, Warkworth, Alnmouth, Alnwick, Seahouses, Bamborough, Christon Bank, Belford, Beal (for Holy Island), Tweedmouth, Berwick. Everywhere the railway lines ran they were bound to meet castles, battlefields and holy places because Northumberland is a county with a long and troubled history. Lucky man, my father, to be paid to go puffing his way in a local invention across the very tables of chronicle and story, his cab-window an eye scanning the centuries every day.

Only he, of course, could decide when this railway stuff was due for slow destruction by water-closet. Others in their need snatched up different bumf. And some that appeared at intervals came from a supply of books which mother had bought at sales, and had since been left to moulder under the stairs until disinterred by me and scribbled on or torn by my sisters. When their condition was judged sufficiently deplorable they were banished to out by. You would find by your shirt-tail every day for some weeks a coverless and tampered-with volume which contained the mortal remains of *The Count of Monte-Cristo* or *Villette, John Halifax, Gentleman, The Last of the Barons* or *Inquire Within Upon Everything*. One at a time, of course, and long intervals between the final destruction of the Dumas work and the coming in of the Craik. Each book diminished daily, so it was a curious kind of reading they provided. You went through as many pages as you had time for, tore off your quota and departed. When you were due to take up the story again, very likely someone else had got ahead of you. There were pages missing, gone beyond recall. Well, you picked up the plot as best you might, amused yourself with another fragment of the fiction, and in turn consigned a few more pages to the swirling waters. As people were tearing their way through from the other end as well, you could never hope to know how the tale worked out; and if the thing was powerful enough to stay in your mind, as Monte-Cristo was, in mine, then you had to get yourself another copy. Now actually this is a fairly good method of going through a book for the first time—I heartily recommend its use with this one, which is somewhat designed for the job, you might say.

Not even here, however, nor anywhere, did anything turn up to throw light on the eighteenth century and Doctor Johnson, until my own attempts to write Johnsonese at school shook down a prize and the prize I chose was the *Vicar of Wakefield*. But how did I know about that work? I didn't. All I knew was that Goldsmith was a minor member of Johnson's gang, so that when we were called into the Headmaster's office and told to make our choice from a number of books spread out on a table the moment I spotted this name of Goldsmith I dived for the book. Older prize-winners looked sour at me as the Headmaster praised my selection, and, of course, it was impossible to explain before him that I hadn't made it for swank. Anyway, I'd got it. And it was excellent. I read it quickly, then my father spent some weeks journeying through this true and gentle tale, commenting on it and re-telling especially good bits until it was vivid to all our family.

Johnson's prestige was enhanced in my mind. I argued that if Goldsmith, previously a pretty poor shower, could be so good, then the Doctor must be terrific. But the problems of discipleship to him were no nearer being plain. At this point, my lane took a sudden turning. My enormous meal of Bible-reading must have at last got itself digested; I realized with complete imaginative clarity that the real hero of Granny's Great Book was neither warrior nor king, not Samson or

Solomon, but Jesus. Obvious, of course: we'd always been told so. But such telling is part of the perpetual drip of admonitory remark against which every boy turns up a mental-coat-collar. If I found truth in it now that was because I'd had practice in looking for it in my effort to appreciate Samuel Johnson, and the need which discarded such earlier heroes as Hereward the Wake, Robin Hood and Dick Turpin in favour of the man who won his fights by his use of words, the weapons of the weak. Now this Jesus seemed to show how weakness could overcome the whole world and miraculously transform it by itself being transformed into goodness. This was to me a very novel idea indeed. Goodness was the victorious aggression of the weak. Of course, it was; I could at once think of many instances which proved it. For instance, on a recent Sunday evening prowling over Armstrong Bridge with some of the lads, we noticed a well-dressed woman taking a bag of toffee from her bag and about to sample it. We crowded up on her, and I said boldly, 'Gi's a bit, greedy.' If she had aimed a swipe at me, as would have been natural, we'd have all danced and ducked around her hoping to fluster her into dropping the paper bag, so that we could snatch it up and pelt off. But instead she stopped and very gently and politely handed it round. We stood like oafs one after another blushing as we pulled at the pieces of sticky toffee and tried not to take too much. Oh, yes, she'd won. We walked off defeated, deflated and not even whistling. What beat us was the positive act of yielding, that gave it grace and robbed us of aggression.

Well, I was of the party of the weak now; to be any good to it, I must learn to be good myself. Of course, I couldn't believe that matters were quite so simple, but the Bible story also indicated that when weakness earnestly seeks to transmute itself into goodness, supernatural aid may be forthcoming. I was thinking all this time you see of the pain and misery and hopeless blind conflict in my own little household, and of the bad star which shone so immovably upon its roof. Perhaps I could redeem it by coming to such a peak of virtue that the supernatural powers must take note, and remove their awful mogador from my mother and us all.

My experience of the Christian faith and practice so far had been average for the area. Through the week it cropped up only during the first lesson of the school day, something called Scripture. I don't remember anyone present, either teacher or pupil, taking any notice of that. It fell like a blanket on the class, levelling our attention off to the uniform dullness so suitable for the reception of the more organized boredom of the subjects which really counted. There were no examinations in Scripture. Occasionally at other council schools in the district, a teacher who happened to be an atheist or an agnostic or something equally serious would try to use this first half-hour to counteract the evil influence of Sunday, but my guess is he wouldn't make it. Scripture was dead horse whichever way you flogged it. Sunday, though, was still the Sabbath day, considerably. It was Parents' day, and parents wanted Peace and Quiet. So Peace and Quiet continually menaced all our comings and goings, and were the containers of any ebullience we were unwilling to subdue utterly. Not that the parents went to church in any great numbers. Practically speaking, they had to be childless to do that. For in most houses, the mother's morning was a turmoil of cooking and getting kiddies turned out clean; the father had his hobbies, pigeons, allotments, canaries, rabbits and beer (especially beer), and handyman's jobs which had waited all the week to be done. The heavy Sunday dinner—half a cow, greens, potatoes and Yorkshire, lashings of rice pudding to follow, which varied in details, but not in character, through all the seasons—was the crown of the day. Rightly, too, for this heap of food marked the triumph of successful parenting, the winnings of the good provider, the achievement of the good cook. When it was over, then was the time for religion—both of them. In working-class circles, Sunday afternoon is traditionally sacred to the worship of Venus and a nice lie-down. Perhaps one reason why the working-class in general is so good-humoured and patient, charitable and unenvious is that they must have been, a great lot of them, conceived on the day of grace. Obviously it is a convenience in these small houses to get the children out of the way. So that's where the secondary religion of Christ comes in handy. As soon as a babe can toddle that far, Sunday school is the destination. When the quarter's enormous dinner-time was over, every street showed a drift of white pinafore and pink frilly dresses (if it was summer), the hot shine of hard straw hats on the knicker-bockered boys. The groups in every avenue moved slowly and sedately through the dinner-scented sunshine, the sedateness being due to repletion rather than to any pious anticipation of the functions they were about to take part in. They converged on the main road, making something of a procession or pilgrimage of youth there, and were gradually sucked into the side-doors of seven churches. The wide road was then left bare to the gleam of tramlines and the multiple stare of blank-blinded shop windows.

Already I had been a pretty regular attendant at all seven of these Sunday schools each by turn. I tried them all not out of any queer passion for savouring doctrinal differences, but

71

as I was moved by advance reports of treats and outings with which each church competed against the others. If the Baptists were about to put on a better do than the Primitive Methodists, then I switched myself and sometimes my sisters over to Baptism. When Baptism began to go broke, I was a Presbyterian. My parents didn't worry over which sect I was hitched to on any particular Sunday: my mother because she thought their differences unimportant and what they agreed about most valuable, my father because he was a sceptic himself and lent his weight to religion only on behalf of such simpletons as needed a fairy tale to keep them straight (that included me).

But now that I was dedicated as a warrior on the side of weakness, I must begin cleaning up my church-going habits. No more dodging the collection, so as to save a copper for sweets. I dropped in a whole penny rather ostentatiously because the teacher had developed a habit of watching me closely to see that I didn't take anything out—and as a brand-new fellow-Christian of his, I wanted *some* credit. There was the matter of the texts, too. Every Sunday we were handed a little card bearing some incomprehensible phrase or other embowered in daisies, pansies or roses. These were proofs that 'we'd bin', as they say on the dart-board. The children of more austere families couldn't play truant because they wouldn't have that week's text to show when they got home. So, of course, I swopped mine with them, usually for cigarette cards. Why wasn't I a truant? Sometimes I was, not often, because I had the civic duty of seeing that my sisters got there, and I was my father's son in the matter of any truancy of theirs. But to me now, in my new mood, texts were treasures, to be taken home, studied and hoarded with reverence between the pages of the great Bible.

When the kids returned from Sunday School and their increasing noise began to register within the bedroom walls, it was time for the wives of the district to come out of any cocoon of connubial love they'd spun themselves into and take up the role of mother again. Each in her separate privacy repeated the motions of all the rest as though the children's return was a sort of muezzin-call to temporarily lapsed motherhood. The late-loved lass stirred away from her lord, relinquished the fragment of honeymoon that still regularly came to her, and got up to find her skirt and shoes in a room dimmed from the brilliant day by pulled curtains or the dropped venetian blind. Perhaps she'd come to the back-door at once if the young ones were too clamorous. There she'd stand or lean for a while, still languid from her loving, her hair mussed up, the flesh of her cheeks fallen slack, a greasy

72

look about her temples and the under eyelid showing a slight thickening—the very picture of woman well-used, and content that she was.

Ay, but that was for five minutes or not much more. Then back to the oven with tarts and cakes to make for tea, a varied selection because it was still Sunday and her family were willing to eat till they bust as long as it was. Her husband would get up when tea was ready, having caught up on some of the arrears of rest always owing to him; and now it would be very pleasant to have all the household in their Sunday best together to be able to cut into a succession of home-cooked confections, to see them disappear with manifest appreciation and to know that they were obviously doing all present a world of good. The cheese or the sausage rolls were followed by rhubarb or gooseberry or red currant or blaeberry tarts; these by Yorkshire cheesecake, jam sponge or fruit, and a great heap of scones. When you'd got through that lot you were fed, by God.

In my new mood of Sabbath seriousness, after tea I avoided my pals in favour of a lonely meditative walk through the parks. We were lucky where we lived in the matter of access to public parks. One short street led from the Avenues to Heaton Road; the far side of Heaton Road for a stretch broke into the great rookery of Heaton Hall; and behind the Heaton Hall grounds, along one side of the Ouseburn Valley, lay two parks, both public, and continuous, except for the slight interruption of a leafy, stone-walled lane. From the second of these parks you emerged into a main road, crossed it, and could immediately sink yourself into the scented shade of the famous Jesmond Dene. Of course, when I say that I was solitary on these summer evenings, I mean in myself; the whole way along the main paths was a regular parade of people in their stiff best clothes. The soft thud and scrape of so many footfalls brought almost to unison by the mere fact of their multitude and the identity of their makers' purpose made a kind of slow march of it which imposed the collective step on my own. When I became aware of this, or irritated by it, I'd weave and dart my way ahead for a minute or so. Then some portion of the Sunday host was fragmentarily aware of me. What they would see was a plump chubby-faced boy in a Norfolk jacket and knickerbockers, black stockings and heavy boots, the face downward-looking and possibly frowning under a flat straw hat or the 'cady' worn throughout the working-class, from Glasgow Green to Casey Court, by Lenin and the Australian cricketers. There were plenty others of my kidney in that parade but not on their own, and not, I

73

must have flattered myself, concerned like me with Higher Things.

Keeping in step without effort the parade wound by two bowling-greens, mathematical swards scribbled on by tree-shadows, and watched by a terrace on which stood a huge aviary holding up the dial of a southward-looking clock; it skirted flower-beds of painfully formal calceolaria, scarlet geranium, lobelia, or a sort of clay boil bursting through turf to shatter into certified bush-roses; it sank and wound into leafier paths where midges monopolized every spare sun-beam and the humble-bee rolled from bloom to bloom on the vibrating iris which miraculously supports its bulk. As I strolled, thinking, I reached out to pull a leaf from each separate kind of plant, bush or tree my hand came near to; these I crushed up in my palm and smelled from time to time to note the difference in the sappy aroma each addition made—a thoroughly Johnsonian habit, had I but known it. What I was thinking about was some very old problems. Why must there be pain and evil in the world? Were they con-sequences of one another? Could we by understanding and demonstrating the relationship bring about their end?

Nearly every park-bench I passed by had on it and round it groups of young men and women who were held by an hilarious and teasing interest in one another which had an under-edge of uneasy purpose to it—was this purpose sin? Were they being drawn under the midge-dance of their point-less repartee into a path not only forbidden, but very justly gin-trapped with disease, accident and misery, all natural consequences of sin? That old man, hobbling along on two sticks, his back humped out as though a tremendous weight had recently fallen across his shoulders—what sin could have brought down that great clout on him? A little way back where the throng was thickest, it suddenly broke step and parted. That was to let through a long basket-work invalid-carriage on which a waxen young lady lay prone, her eyes twisting up to the sky or the tree-fringe to avoid the glances of pity and curiosity coming her way—was she a late deep sinner? No, this could not be. Such folk must be suffering as Jesus did, for the sins of others. They were like many a wife in our parts who regularly wore a black eye because her hus-band was given to an untidy belligerence when drunk. But perfect love, my text said, could cast out sin. This beautifully simple statement was a turning-point in my meditations since at that time I had not spotted the cunning qualification of its only adjective. No, I was ready to rejoice in such a rush of universal tenderness as must set the whole world to rights. The excitement of the thought caused my feet to stumble on

74

the gravel, the sun-spangled evening, its bright faces and its vistas of blossom and greenery, shook as my eyes watered. It could be done, you see; Christ had shown the way. I felt in my pocket to touch the cheap metal crucifix which I'd bought out of the pennies from some returned beer-bottles and which had to be concealed from them that jeer—this was the symbol of the new lad I was.

And then it was natural to pass on to day-dreaming. I daydreamed of the triumphs to be gained out of my own moral perfection when I'd achieved it; I saw my family brought miraculously into concert, all nice as ninepins to one another; my mother's lameness banished, skipping the details of how— by prayer, perhaps, or by the meteor-descent of some interpolating angel; my sisters happy because they were freed now of the terrors they endured during the ugly husband-wife battles they witnessed and which were only one stage off bloodshed, if that; I saw even further a general spread of ecstatic and enthusiastic kindness among all our folks until the whole network of shabby streets and work-torn humanity about them were lit in the undying sun of a permanent Easter morn—that was a dream that could be; for I could feel inside me the stretch and leap of a common triumph almost, everywhere almost, ready to be free.

But to be practical now, where could I begin? The descent to the practical, always like going down cold cement steps in bare feet, led as ever to the discovery of some object of utility which must have mocked the imagination except that the imagination of visionaries does not include an awareness of the comical. I decided, very serious and grave, that the proper down-to-earth beginning of my crusade was a cleansing of the home. My mother, you see, was letting things drift. Her pride was declining into mere reminiscence most times; only now and again were her energies equal to a total onslaught on the accumulation of neglected duties. Usually, when you came into the living-room, you'd see that the table was spread with newspapers, even those stained with yesterday's spillings; no one had cleared away the half-loaf, the margarine in its paper, the pot of jam or the fly-infested tin of condensed milk. Discarded garments and dirty towels heaped up on the sofa; there were miscellaneous boots about the fender; the hearthrug, which had a hole in it, badly needed a shaking; whatever object had come to rest on the mantelshelf had a coating of dust or a streak of smut from some boisterous fire-puffing when last there was a cross-wind in the chimney. Even the once-gorgeous Front Room had subsided to junk-shop state. The introduction to it of the big brass-knobbed bed and of an iron cot, the after-disorder of four sleepers not regularly repaired, made it frowsty, bed-fluffed, unusable by day. Well, my idea was to make all this place as clean and comfortable as I remembered it used to be.

I had a model to inspire me: the prototype of the spotless working-class home was not far away. Many a morning or mid-day on my way to school, supposing I chose the Sixth Avenue route, I'd be rambling along stooped in thought, dream or the mere anticipation of coming boredom when a rich Northumbrian voice might rattle on my ear-drum, 'Willum, straighten up!' I did so at once, and turned a placatory glance to the door or window where the trim-bosomed figure of my Aunt Mary Jane must have appeared. She was a tidier-upper, she was. Her whole life was a fearful struggle against the Apollyon of Dirt, or 'Dort' as she pronounced it. Anybody but herself would have said she was the victor. Not her. She could see 'dort' on surfaces that to the uninstructed eye had been polished down to a new skin of cleanliness. 'Dort' was always creeping in behind her, following after her broom and breeding even where the duster had just left off. She fought it constantly, and to the nearest thou. of obliteration—it was still there, that is, to her remorseless eye. Everyone else thought her house a fair dazzler. And I don't mean by comparison with such as ours, but with fairly-weighted competitors. The working-class wife who really goes in for cleanliness, as plenty do, especially if she has no children, keeps a home which easily outshines any in the country. People of the other classes have largely lost their standards in this matter, perhaps because they relied for so long on domestic servants and are used to the superficial wipe-round of work done for wages or by themselves in the heroism of economy. The true graft of scrupulous dirt-hatred is not there. In the middle-class house one is nearly always aware of a latent dinginess; without looking closely it is a safe bet that the corners, the places in shadow, have been skipped; the swift wipe of polish doesn't really cover up the lack of scrubbing; there are traces of haste and slick deceiving about—as there will be in the grub when you get it. As you pick about delicately among the morsels assembled according to B.B.C. or Woman's Page recipe, all you can do is to reflect that the mistress was in the garden and the maid was just going to the pictures and these facts stared you in the face from underneath the furniture the moment you entered the house.

Aunt Mary Jane was a true countrywoman of the old type. Though she lived in a town near to shops of all sizes and capacities she dealt with a country carter who solemnly booked her order, drove up the street to a store, bought what she wanted, and carefully delivered it one week later on his next round. I don't suppose she ever saw a film in her life; and gardening she left to her husband. But the house—'hoose' she called it—the hoose was her supreme concern. When I was allowed inside it, I had the sensation of coming into a glass palace. Breathe and you left a stain. Uncle Bill always arrived by the back-door, where he took off his boots and stepped in his socks from one bit of newspaper to another until he arrived at his seat left side of the hearth. There he sat most evenings, his feet still on newspaper, because they were sweaty and might stain the polished surface of the linoleum. He was a road-sweeper employed by the city corporation, a large man somewhat John Bullish in his side-whiskers and the deep weathering he got from his outdoor work but with no arrogance at all, no, gentle, soft-natured, easily hurt, his strength a menace to none and his slow broad speech an acceptance of the right of more forward-thrusting mortals to have their own way, always provided they didn't push him too far out of his road. Each evening he was allowed a couple of pipefuls of tobacco, not more because it was a dirty habit and costly. But as he smoked Rubicon twist, it was easy to let the pipe out now and then so as to make it last while he went slowly through the main news in the *Evening Chronicle*. His wife had the births-and-deaths page. Between them was a kitchen range so jetty-black and twinkling even the coals burning in the grate looked as if they'd been through the shoe-shine's hands before getting there, and the flames could admire the ballet of their reflections in a long steel fender bright as all the swords of Damascus—that is, when it wasn't covered in newspaper as it was all day.

Aunt Mary Jane studied the deaths. Any of the Northumbrian names, Charlton or Forster or Twizell say, set her speculating on who the deceased could be. She and her husband were related to half the clans on the Border; she couldn't realize that names once localized had gone into the city melting-pot and were becoming meaningless as indications of the owner's clan-membership. For example, when my father complained once that a watch-maker called Forster had made an unsatisfactory job of mending his watch—'Ay,' says she, "the Forsters were always a bad lot. Ye should ha' knaan bettor than take it theor.' You could see she was thinking not of the millions of Forsters there are now, but of the small group of families so-named who specialized in Border dirty work two or three centuries ago. So if she read now that a certain Thomas Young had died in the village of Longbenton aged only nineteen, she'd recall that her husband had a cousin Young who had a son, who went to work in the pit by Benton and could it be him, d'ye think? Uncle Bill agreed it might be. But he should have heard something since his stretch of road took him half-way to Benton? Ay, well, he'd ax any Benton fellow he saw tomorrow. At that he stopped to think back for any slight clue that might have been dropped to indicate which Young this was that had got his death so early and so near to Bill's own territory. But Mary Jane was further down the column now. He sucked on his dead pipe, perhaps reached down to light a spill between the bars. At once her eyes leaped to his action, in dread lest he drop any ash or sparks on that speckless fender. So they sat most evenings in this showcase of a room surrounded by reflecting surfaces and under the presidency of a proud and glittering grandfather clock which always seemed to me to be saying 'No dort, no dort'.

Well, I tried to introduce some of this shining order into our own ragtime establishment. It was harder work than ever I'd thought it. It didn't last either. Somebody was always untidying what I'd just tidied. I got vexed with my sisters on this score. Nevertheless, it might have been that my efforts really did have some effect, certainly for a period rows became much less frequent and for this unwonted peace I felt entitled to take the credit. But the spell of cleanliness didn't stay dominant for very long. All too soon the old shuttlecock of practised discord was flying back and forth again and all parties took up their regular positions for it. I'd come home some evening to find battle had commenced. There was my father sitting clean and tense in his fireside chair, his workshirt fastened at the neck with a discoloured metal stud, his sleeves rolled up and baring the arm-muscles which bulked under his fair skin. He never slumped in his seat, but sat poised on his buttocks, able to rise in a moment and perhaps to follow up his last contemptuous phrase with the threat of a blow. Sensing that, mother had retreated to the door. From there, flushed in her anger and afraid, she'd continue to produce masterpieces of repartee keeping the shuttlecock in the air. My sisters sat on the neutral ground of the couch in their nightgowns crying soft or loud from wary eyes as the action proceeded. Now I slunk into the armchair of the opposite neutral ground and the pattern was complete.

The kitchen about this time and for many years was papered in red, a red, angry room, its atmosphere sore with the frequent cut and thrust of murderous argument. Endless, useless banging of words, the quiver and sting of home-truths hurled regardless of audience as these two who were once in love but who never had any understanding of each other, tore down their illusions and came to a shameful nudity of soul

78

before their children. As I listened my own anger, male like my father's, rose in me. If I'd had the power I would have willingly jumped up to wipe the sneer off his handsome face or to smack the smart answer back into my mother's teeth. And then my own fear, female as my mother's, tugged me down and I wanted to rush her out of the room before she said the last unforgivable thing which must bring her antagonist springing to his feet. But at that moment, she said it: there was the white flash of his rising full into the gas-glare, a crescendo of crying from the sofa, mother's flurry to get round the door, and the murderous blow we feared was suspended while all died down. The kids in their pink night-gowns shuffled off to bed like dismissed supers after a rehearsal; the man in his anger sat again and reached for his cold pipe; I bent down to undo my bootlaces—the signal-board was off, red light out, life could proceed to a clear line again.

Next to cleanliness in my programme was godliness. The practical difficulties of being good at my time of life were pretty nearly insuperable it seemed to me. I was obviously a case where supernatural intervention was necessary. I could at least pray. Pray I did; in fact prayer began going up in large chunks nightly from the little back bedroom below that into which one November night the spirit of propagation descended to start the small tick of my earliest animation. I prayed in 'Our Fathers' linked on an interminable mental rosary, one for each name I could think of, and a clincher in the name of domestic peace generally. The repetition hushed me into a near-hypnotic state so that on the brims of my eye-lids, especially if it was a moonlit night, I could just begin to make out the sudden silvery confusion of a great descent; another second and the slant and glitter of moonshine splinter-ing darkness would steady into the winged and robed figure brilliant with celestial benevolence which my imagination conjured from the heavens. But then my eyes opened. The room was empty; the prayer unregarded. Cold, broken moons swung in the glass of the picture frames; a sullen salt of moon-dust sprinkled the top of a chest of drawers, but that was all the magic there was. No salvation there. My eyes tired; I heard distant voices raising the drunkards' anthem of 'Nellie Dean', (then just out); the ordinary tumble of metal down the junction and what next I knew was the dingy day of school, work, drink and squabbling.

Discouraging this. Yet it was the cleanliness front which broke first. One afternoon just as I had finished a great tidying-up, my father came in from work. I hoped for some favourable comment from him on the improved look of the

home and who had done it. But before he had time to take
it in, my sisters began throwing cushions about. I reproved
them, priggishly, of course. Up came his loud voice, 'Let
them be. What d'ye think ye're playing at? A Jessie fussing
about the hoose?' I shrank inside. A Jessie, a little girl doing
mammy's housework. He was right, of course. I had the
instinct to feel that. Not even for the purest of motives is it
good to make a lassie of yourself if you aren't one by nature,
except for the temporary run of some unusual emergency,
that only. I dropped my campaign of cleanliness-in-the-home,
and the danger of my becoming an unnatural competitor with
the other sex in a matter which belongs to their dominion
thereupon, and for henceforth, ever after, ceased.

My religious meditations were also beginning to bang into
the buffers. Perhaps another phase of growth was asserting
itself, the period of purely vegetable amplifying and putting
on of beef and muscle which very often comes on a youngster
who has lately been getting a bit too bright mentally. But what
I remember of it was my discovery that the religious—includ-
ing myself?—were not all admirable. During a few rather
self-conscious attendances at church on Sunday evenings (self-
conscious because children did not go to church services unless
they were taken) I became aware that the main supporters of
religion in our district were people whom we hardly regarded
as belonging to our community. These were the dull, the safe,
the unthreatened from without or within—what need had
they of this religion? They were white-collar men, a lot of
them, who wore the gloss of subservience that came from their
physical softness and their unhealthy proximity to the boss;
or they were drapers, grocers, insurance agents; or they were
the kind of working-man who remains a hat-toucher and a
blackleg even in the towns out of an inherited complex. They
were all folk that could come singly by the corner-ends with-
out awakening any enthusiasm or interest even, and put
altogether like this they were not impressive except in a
negative and daunting way. No, it was disappointing to look
round these rows of hymn-singers and sermon-hearkeners.
Where were the publicans and sinners, the black sheep come
to repentance, the weak ones whose only hope of finding
strength was in the comradeship of religious affirmation? I
began to see that things must have been different in Biblical
times, and to guess that now Christianity was become a
stinker's creed used by the kind of weak who are careful and
cunning, able to perceive the social value of proclaiming their
every meanness as a virtue, so that a diminished generosity, for
instance, they call charity; a complete lack of it, thrift; a
withering of the convivial spirit, sobriety; of the concupiscent

one, chastity; and generally, whenever their horse didn't dare gallop, to claim the credit of reining it in. Ay, well, somehow here I could feel, a great idea was being shat upon. *Weakness becoming goodness is collectively strong.* But they struck out the collective bit, contracted out of comradeship, and made it read *My weakness is goodness and is therefore strong.* Because the rest of us half-believed them, they were strong, the miserable bastards. Then, if Christianity had become their weapon, it was obviously no use to my mother's son, still less to my father's. In fact, I saw the whole dream receding into history like the chivalry of Robin Hood or the daring of Dick Turpin. It did not live now.

Such impressions and glimpses of the wheels going round accumulated upon me then without my being able to think them out clearly. So I cannot say precisely how they ripened in me and there was nothing dramatic in it when they did. One Sunday evening I was mooning about alone on the corner-end. It was getting dark, a blowy sort of darkness which piled up over the western roof-tops and was dense towards the open end of the street which the lamp-lighter hadn't yet reached. I stood watching the tiny star he carried above his shoulder winking along; I waited for the successive bursts of light his star-wand touched to greatness; and casually, purposelessly, playing with the crucifix in my pocket. I took it out and began levering the Jesus from his cross. He came off easily enough, the lean silvery figure, effigy of self-fraud if anything. I suppose I had some idea of finding a novel use for it but nothing occurred to me. There was a drain at the kerb by my feet—I bent down and let Jesus slip through the grating. There was no supernatural manifestation as yet another of his gods forsook him—he slid into the black liquid and vanished. His cross was a fraud too, soft white metal which broke easily in my fingers. I threw it piece by piece at the street-lamp, each piece flashing in the light as it tapped on the pane and the last cracking a triangular piece of glass which presently fell out. An ensuing draught set the gas-mantle wobbling; its light shook all around me like a web. I stepped out of it, and set off running along the dark pavements.

Chapter Nine

GUY FAWKES LIGHTS UP TWO
WORLDS

Luckily I had never allowed anything of this religious phase
of mine to show on me during school hours. Neither its com-
ing nor its passing could have been noticed there. No doubt
there were moments when I endeavoured to put a little extra
fervour into the singing of 'Strong Son of God, Immortal
Love', or 'All Things Bright and Beautiful' with which we
alternately began the day, 'Strong Son' if wet, 'Bright and
Beautiful' when it was, but as my voice was not musical
enough to register any emotional quality, the effort was lost
on one and all. As far as school went I was no different from
my pals, not for a long time. Each examination found me out-
side the first ten, but in the first twenty-five of a class which
numbered between fifty and sixty. That was enough to secure
a regular move up every six months, but not to call any un-
welcome attention to my prowess from teachers or school-
mates. As to the great virtue they gave all the best prizes
for, regular-attendance-and-punctuality, it is simplest to say
that I was never there when I could find a convincing excuse
for not going and when I had to be my arrival was regularly
first, second or third last.

There was a school bell which tolled for some five minutes
in the mornings, a peculiarly flat despondent sound, not
urgent, not very loud, though it carried all over the Avenues,
and it always seemed as if it was meant to go on forever. Then
all at once, it didn't. And the tempo it had been upholding, so
weary and dutiful, right for the time of day, slid into one long
moment. In fact all the motions of the morning, without a
metronome now, congealed slightly, so it seemed to me. The
silence clung to horses and trams and was especially impeding
on my legs. I had to run round the whole eastern face of the
brick barracks, past many class-room windows before I got
to the playground where the lines of boys had formed up
ready for their march into the hall. Far too often when I got
to it, the playground was empty. I had to push my way through
more of this sluggish morning air, going hard and panting,
before I caught up the last of my comrades either on the stairs
or, final chance, crossing the hall. Miss that and I was a pro-

claimed defaulter. After the hymns and 'Our Father' when the teacher had time to attend to me, I'd get a belting for being late. This was delivered on the hands with a leather strap and you didn't want it too early if the day was cold.

The week's curriculum, I fancy, must have been a bit of a conundrum to all concerned. Why were we learning or not learning these things? Of course, reading, writing, arithmetic have their own sense to them, like sewing, knitting and cooking in a smaller world, but drawing, but history, but grammar, botany, singing, geography, geometry, recitation— what mortal use could they be to the likes of us? Our parents said, to help us to get better jobs. Most of us didn't want better jobs. We despised people who came home clean from their work and had in consequence a somewhat unreal and un-affirmed look, lacking the used coarseness of full men. Our teachers said it was a fine thing to be educated. Yes, but they were educated themselves; we looked at them as we had looked for many a jaundiced hour, and if there was any fine-ness upon them, we were not the ones to see it, not us. The fact is, not they nor anybody could say plainly what we were being educated for. In a few schools up and down the country, teaching is a simple matter because the pupils have a reason-ably foreseeable future which can be contemplated cheer-fully. They have waiting for them the same assured position in adult society that their parents had. The teacher must pre-pare them for that position by the appropriate character-conditioning, initiation into the peculiar code of behaviour which is the mark of their kind, and a laying-on of the gold leaf of culture to make them look worthy of the job already picked for them. In some other schools the communication of a technique to pre-selected aspirants is the chief thing. But our lot of kids were going to be just ordinary workers. They'd be inferior in class-status even to their teachers. Now what character, what code of behaviour, what culture is appropriate to the worker?

They hold revolutions about that question, in some places. You couldn't expect our teachers to have the answer. Of course, they hadn't, so in practice the school unconsciously orientated its teaching towards the exceptions among us. Some of us were destined in the ordinary course of luck to land up in gaol or on the streets, some were going to be lifted up into a higher social class. How many of these latter? That was the point. Our school was doing very well it con-sidered, by the only practical test that existed, if it managed to raise the proportion of pupils capable of winning scholar-ships and getting thereby possible passports to Better Things. True, we had some teachers who disliked this dominance of the competitive examination. They often made individual efforts to counter its effect. Yet these could never add up to an acceptable alternative policy. Always the pride that prevailed in this working-class school was that it succeeded in turning out less recruits for the working-class than any other of its kind in the district. That less was still the majority, mind you, a great crowd that stayed on for two or three years after the scholarship culling was over and were then worked upon and encouraged to flash what talents they had. But the school's official boast was not of them. The names in blue and red displayed on a whole row of rolls-of-honour hanging in the hall were all those of educable small fry that had taken kindly to a scholastic bunk-up and been duly dispatched to the sphere of Higher Education. A queer system, once one thinks of it; and though it never bothered us at the time, it might account for some of the pointlessness of our schooldays and for the relatively trivial impression they made on us.

Of course, this great matter of the scholarship examinations, the annual catharsis of the crammed, did not confront any pupil until he was approaching the age of eleven. At least, it did not in most cases. A few children had parents who were ambitious on their behalf, supervised their homework and pestered them about the progress they were making at their lessons. Not mine, not my mates. For us these early schooldays crawled across the calendars and it was rare that any parental prod urged us to make a race of it. Through the department called Infants, on to Juniors and upstairs to Seniors, our little company moved through classes and classrooms that were so similar you could call them the same and be near enough right. Nine till twelve, two to four or four-thirty, these were the hours of petrifaction. They were subdivided, it is true, and there were squares drawn on white paper to illustrate the fact, into hours and half-hours called Arithmetic, Grammar, Drawing and the like. Sometimes new ones, Geography as it might be or Composition, came along. Ah, but we veterans knew from of old that they'd all be the same thing essentially. We met them all with the same dull fortitude and brightened only for the various interruptions that came to them.

The chief and only regular official interruption was Playtime. For a quarter of an hour every morning and every afternoon, the screw was loosened. At those times the two gravelly tarmac lakes outside which had been still and so silent you could hear the flutter of sparrows' wings as well as their wild chirping, instantly filled with a whooping, darting throng that multiplied itself in constantly changing combinations and re-combinations like a sort of gnat-dance of kiddy, or like a

84

working model of the interior of the atom, electrons in knickerbockers weaving and charging among cloth-capped neutrons, forming into groups or breaking off again on some principle of attraction and repulsion that no bystander was likely to find understandable at sight. After the first couple of minutes most of it was settling down though you might never notice it. Games were beginning to emerge. Not organized ones, luckily, that ossification of the spirit of play had not yet set in. Backs were being bent for the ancient sport of Montykitty; counting rhymes were being said and a fist struck at every figure or word ('One potato, two potato, three potato, four; five potato, six potato, seven potato, raw; and out goes he like a dirty—rotten—dish—clout, OUT—GOES—HE') so as to pick teams for a wild variety of Prisoner's Base; on the school steps, two champions were already holding the fort against all comers. These things for those who liked the rough-and-tumble, as I did myself. There was no compulsion about what we did. Some lads spent the whole playtime in swopping items from their collections; some in teasing; some in patient efforts to destroy at least one little bit of school. But where a group stood mainly still, it had to endure the meteor showers of the perpetually mobile, then abruptly at the sound of a whistle all activity was sucked down to one place. There was a general coalescence as of flies on a cow-pat, with a few outriders still to make it, and the citizenry of school became countable again ready to be drawn indoors under a diminuendo of chatter.

And now we had only accident to look to for relief. The least departure from routine was welcome. It was Dictation, say, but outside the day had darkened for dirty weather. Perhaps there was old snow on the window-sills, shrunk and salt-like stuff pitted with soot-specks like a sort of poor man's ermine. The long panes above it began to picture a pervasion of yellow wreaths upon a slate sky. We were interested, of course. Perhaps somebody's chimney was a-fire? No, it was fog. Good—in fact, better still. If it got worse over the dinner break, mebbe we wouldn't be able to see our way back to school. We watched it until our eyes when re-called by the teacher saw a very dim class-room indeed. 'Please, miss, I can't see,' somebody would say hopefully. But he was premature. Teacher could see. Dictation resumed its dreary way. All the same, it *was* getting darker. Several lads had to be reprimanded for lowering their cheeks to desk-level as they poked their pens along. And the windows showed a dingy yellow backed on purple, the colour of bruises going off. In the end, Teacher had to send someone to fetch the caretaker in order to have the gas-lamps lit. Dictation was off pro tem.

85

the teacher who was to play us out had opened the lid of the piano out in the hall. 'In the Shadows' was the tune she played. To its measure we stepped out smartly, and the great windows of the hall crowded as they were with billowing night-clouds still day-throated rolled one by one away from us as we marched. We were free again and the streets were ours.

That was the broad pattern of school life up to the age of eleven. It was the same for all of us, except that a few of the less-bright missed the regular six-monthly promotions from one class to another and were left behind to do their time over again. As far as I remember, nobody felt any particular shame in that. We weren't competing; there was no obvious advantage in moving up to another class where sums were harder and words got longer; and among us if you weren't specially clever there was nothing odd about that for most likely neither were your parents, your sisters or your brothers. As for your future prospects, well, in any case, the probability was that you would be going into a job very like the one your old man had—you didn't want to be too bright for that. You see, in this school, as on Tyneside generally, almost everyone was working-class. Our fathers worked on the railway, in the factory, in the shipyard, most of them, and you get the scale of it for this area if you reflect that a factory or shipyard employing five thousand men would be unlikely to count more than two hundred and fifty middle-class folk among them. Up to now none of my pals had been thus favoured in their domestic origin. But while the selection for scholarship training was going on amongst us, I did strike up a friendship with someone strangely outside the corner-gangs.

It happened over a deal in foreign stamps. I'd got a selection on approval, the terms being that if you sold so many you were allowed to keep a proportion for yourself, free. All were interested to the extent of grabbing the sheets and pawing them over, but money was very rare in forthcoming. When I'd got them back and was coming away from the group, a boy called Edmund asked if he could have a look. Edmund was a boy who usually never entered one's thoughts. Rather cissy he looked in shorts and a college cap, so clean, too, that it was unpleasant to grab him since he felt like a girl. He knew something about stamps, though, was careful in making his selection and chose well but expensively. What he picked amounted to a whole shillings-worth. I stopped him at the point where he was about to take the stamps off the sheets. I'd seen blokes like him before, I thought, and I wasn't allowing tick. But it shook me when he casually produced his shilling and handed it over. So far I'd never met a boy who could calmly turn a shilling out of his pocket and spend it on impulse just like that. I thought he must have pinched it out of his mother's purse—a thing I'd done myself before now. But he was so calm about his wealth—he left me staring. He invited me to come and see his stamp-collection and I agreed to that at once.

Edmund, it turned out, lived in the relatively posh area north of the Avenues. Immediately after school we slipped round Tenth Avenue back lane and crossed several hushed and desperately clean streets where such children as were about had an unnatural tendency to disappear indoors. I was regretting having come when Edmund quietly let fall the astonishing information that his father was a detective. I looked at him queerly, for this was hardly to be believed. But he didn't blench, or run on to other phrases as a liar most likely would. It must be true. It put him very much in credit —me, too, for knowing him.

When he indicated his house, I saw that it was a semi-detached, with both an upstairs and a downstairs, a tiny garden both back and front and a toy greenhouse. We were met at the door by his mother. She was large and blonde and pink, very smartly dressed, although a brief pinafore indicated that she was a working housewife of sorts, she smelt of scent, had pearly ear-rings and a thin gold bangle—altogether a Ma-de-luxe. She set us down to a glass of milk and a pink iced bun each, and when we'd finished—not before—brought out the stamp collection. It was immense. Pounds and pounds had been spent on it. My own ramshackle and poverty-stricken accumulation went down so far before it that I at once cancelled the idea of ever showing mine in return.

But all his possessions were on a similar scale. I considered his father must be wealthy, not allowing for the fact that Edmund was an only child and focus for all the adult spending power that was about. During several visits, I never met this father because at six prompt, Edmund had to sit down to do his homework, whereupon I left. He made a face over this, but that was all. In fact, what bothered me while I was there and kept our friendship intermittent was that we were so mysteriously controlled. His parents did not bully him; they did not obtrude in our play. But there was a sort of ambience of parenthood in his neighbourhood. You could not strike away from it out to the open street, or be driven out of its way. No, it yielded us boys a place, with a politeness of invitation such as I had never so far encountered, so you took that place and were then over-comfortable, full-legalized, but observed. That made me uneasy.

I never invited Edmund to our place, as I did all the rest of my pals: that would not have done somehow. They, my pals, were quite indifferent to Edmund. To them, he must have seemed a creature of another sex. Not that he was girlish in physique or tendency, but his speech, and his way of dressing, the atmosphere of him, was so strangely different from our own you tended to set him down as a sort of girl of another species. He interested me, though, periodically. He had read quite a lot, was intelligent, had that easy taking-it-for-granted air with which he chucked away his shilling, and these qualities, or the unexpected sum they made, brought me back at times to do another smelling around at him. Probably I was in need at that time of a friendship more intimate than the gangs afforded.

If so, this wasn't it. One day when all boydom was being stirred by the near advent of Guy Fawkes' night, Edmund pulled me aside and in his quiet way told me that his father had bought a terrific supply of fireworks—would I come along and help to set them off? Many times I had dreamt of some such windfall coming to us, well, here it was, not directly to me, but more truly after the manner in which dreams come to life, arriving obliquely into my neighbourhood. My mother was the connoisseur of dreams curiously fulfilled— I told her about this one. That was unwise, because when she had got over her pleasure in the matter, she sensed that this was a social occasion and insisted that I clean up for it. Therefore, most unsuitably for a Guy Fawkes' night, I wore a clean face and a new collar. In that get-up and the cool Edmund's company, I turned away from the excited and rowdy Avenues towards his street.

Even on that night it looked undisturbed; bland asphalt flowing unruffled between pavements still innocent of kids. But in the back-gardens, underneath trees that still held back a rag or two of sunset, there seemed to be a number of fugitive and separate activities going on. 'They're making bonfires everywhere,' Edmund pointed out, feeling my lack of excitement. But the street was bare of them; you could see clean along the swell of its asphalt to where the northern sky came down and on its pallor the Bear was trying to print itself.

We got the usual welcome of the bun and the glass of milk from the gracious lady whose whim it was to appear so improbably as Edmund's Ma, but he couldn't eat. When would his father be home, he wanted to know. I realized that there'd be no fireworks till then. Glum outlook. Ma-de-luxe said several times that we shouldn't be so impatient, half an hour would soon pass. I bet I looked forlorn myself recognizing once again the silly-cow-you-can-do-nothing-with look which sooner or later shows up on every nice woman, and others.

Then she said that we could look at the fireworks—if our hands were clean!

They certainly were a proud assembly, those fireworks, such a wealth of outsize rockets, roman candles of a truly papal rotundity, catherine wheels, flower-pots, rains and showers, all of a size and magnificence never before seen by the likes of us except behind plate-glass windows. And we were actually touching them! Then we started counting them. As we did so, we could hear the distant bangs from other quarters where the fun had already begun. 'What about letting off one or two?' I suggested. Edmund didn't answer properly; he mumbled something and rushed off into the other room to see if it was time for his father to be home yet. Alas! it seemed that it was father's fireworks we were touching.

Well, you can imagine the rest of that evening. Edmund's father turned up, prompt I should think; we never doubted that he would. A clean-shaven dark pipe-smoking man with very clean hairy hands and a speech so genteel to my ears it defeated his efforts to produce a masculine growl. Very skilfully he set rockets in bottles, and they all went up; his competence in the management of a catherine wheel was certainly great; he never overturned a roman candle; and when he put a match to the orderly little bonfire you felt he could have told you within a minute or so how long it would burn. Next door and up and down the gardens similar employs were taking place. One heard delighted shrieks of a sort and affable male growls. Edmund too, seemed to be getting some fun out of this, but for me, I had a wan look as of one who has filled his breeches and should be somewhere else.

At one point we were invited to hold a streamer each, and told to be careful. Like a hypnotist's assistant working under notice I stood holding the thing out till its shoot of gold sparks bent and died on the smoky air. I don't think anyone noticed anything wrong with me. Both pink-blonde Ma and dark cleft-chinned father had their eyes on Edmund who, rather wonderfully they felt, was waving his golden rain like a conductor leading a slow movement. Beyond us, and far about us, the atmosphere shuddered and pulsed to other pyrotechnics and it seemed to me that slow hours had passed and all the fun would be over in my own places before I could get away from this ghastly one-man display.

Then it turned out that clever Dad had saved one last rocket to the end. And we never noticed, fancy! Whoosh it went straight for the Pole Star, fell short, and at the end of its arc gently floated four fire-dots on the fall of the sky. It is the only one of the rockets I remember, because it spelt Finis-thank-the-Lord, and though we looked at the embering bon-

90

fire for a bit, it couldn't have been so very long before I was free to go. Like a rocket horizontally aimed I shot past these dead pavements and left not a star behind me.

But the moment I turned into the Avenues, I could see that it wasn't late at all. The fire festival of Fawkes was still on here and in very full swing indeed. At the bottom end of Ninth back-lane a mattress on the bonfire had just caught alight, the dervishes around it jumped and yelled from fiery-smudged faces; Eighth were entrenched within their narrow gardens, hurling Chinese crackers and jumping-jacks at all who passed by; Seventh were engaged in a slanging match because the great pyramid of their fire, crowned with a guy sitting in an arm-chair, had toppled over and was burning against somebody's back door. There were no gorgeous rockets or fat roman candles around these parts. We went in for the cheaper kinds that you got more of. And many a group now were down to squibs. It didn't so much matter so long as you had something to make you one of the crowd. There *was* a crowd, too. Not much hope of getting the offspring early to bed tonight. You could see even the near-toddlers solemnly lighting each other's sparklers from the hot end of the last one to burn out, and there were little girls running wild as they tried to throw lit London Lights into the air. Naturally the excitement I had missed at Edmund's do got me now. But I didn't explore the cross-avenues or look what Third were doing: I made straight for the boozer.

My mother, I thought, was bound to be in the back bar of the Chillingham. I didn't like the place, and never went there except in necessity. This was necessity: I wanted some money to buy fireworks. My God, but it was a chill little place, that back bar, like a Gents seen from the outside. Four small ground-glass windows high up—if you climbed to them and could hang on by your finger-tips and boot-toes long enough, all you saw was the mysterious and oddly fluid black shapes of imbibing crones, above them a scrambled light smear where the gas-globe hung. There was a passage-way of smooth cold concrete and a door on the right with a brass latch so far up the door panel it was difficult to reach up and rattle it. When you succeeded and somebody opened up, you got a glimpse of a counter shut off from the bar by ground glass screens and two or three untidy women drinking at it. They might be laughing but it was witches' laughter, it was laughter against the run of play, for this was a chill and furtive place pushed out of the way by the weight of public disapproval, and it was that disapproval these hags laughed against, uncheerfully.

When I managed to attract her attention and she came out to me, my mother saw at the first glance that she shouldn't

91

inquire how I'd enjoyed myself. She gave a little toss of her head, defiance to whoever or whatever had marred my evening, and she was eager to turn out her coppers so that whatever I had missed could be made up to me. The moment I'd got the money, I urged her to go home. Vaguely she said she was just going when she finished her drink. I said I'd wait for her then, though I was itching to be off. But the door opened again, and there was one of the worst of her boozing pals, the deadly slab-cheeked Ma McGrewin, coming out to give me a penny and try once again to ingratiate herself with me. My amiable fuddle-headed mother was good as lost now, I knew. I added the extra penny to my store, raced off to the fireworks shop, and was soon fully-equipped to take my place in the third world that owned me, that company of the streets who were at one of the peaks of communal pleasure this very night.

Edmund went out of my life. He was one of those selected for scholarship cramming, a good selection it proved since he won his scholarship all right, in fact, I believe he won two. I was rejected, a good rejection too, confirmed fairly regularly in after-life by many other authorities given the opportunity of showing me the door. The chosen assembled in a corner class-room, and settled down in an atmosphere of earnest quiet; the rejects were herded into a somewhat scruffy room next door where chaos and rebellion reigned. Occasionally during our hilarities we might peer through the glass partition at the fifty busy pens toiling away next door; and you might catch one wandering gaze from a misplaced crammee longing to be out of it. Perhaps it was this contrast in our fates that made our lot so wild and would-be tough: we had been judged unfit for educational advancement—were we not then, licensed to be of bad behaviour? If that was it, the circumstances then ruling favoured the attitude demanded by our psychological state. War had been declared during the holidays; a couple of teachers had gone to it, and one of the vacant places was filled by a very young man of little experience and hardly any natural authority. We got him, or he got us, poor fellow.

In no time we discovered that he didn't like belting us. He was one of those who can strike only in anger, and then with no sureness because half of him was in recoil from his own emotion just as it was overwhelming him. A thin gangling young man with a long neck and a large Adam's apple, he seemed to be caught in the act of gulping and this impression was strongest at the very times when he was trying to seem the authentically fearsome figure of authority outraged. Half the class were defying him in various ways, behind his back and all around, as he struggled to deal with the boy before him. That boy was mass-supported, obstinately and cunningly cheeky. The teacher's anger mounted; he whirled round to his desk and pulled out the strap. A stride and he stood over the boy, his Adam's apple working and the strap pulled through his trembling fingers. But he couldn't strike, or if he did it was nothing of a blow and he was so obviously distressed by it, we—and the boy, though he didn't forget to yell— thoroughly enjoyed his upset. Seeing that this was no good, he thought he'd try more humane punishments. Double your homework was one. Now we would have thought that a dirty trick if we'd really had to do what he set. But we didn't, and he hadn't the power to insist. Then he had an idea he might bring a rebel to shame by making him go and sit among the girls. I, myself, was one of the first to come under this sentence. I lumbered out of the boys' aisles grinning and receiving considerable encouragement from my pals and made my way to the only vacant seat on the girls' side of the class.

My new partner promptly shrank from me to the extreme edge of her desk. But presently we were taking peeps at each other. A dark-eyed lassie with ringlets the colour of heather honey and a marvellous softness of cheek and throat, her name Yvonne. It was printed in capitals on her exercise book: YVONNE DAUBIGNY. I knew her name already without having taken any note of it, but now, seeing it on the page set out like that, it struck me that perhaps she was French. Many foreign countries had recently become vivid for us because of the war, and it was instantly exciting to me to think that I might have a little foreigner from an allied country sitting next to me. I whispered to know if she was. She laughed down into her pinafore and darkened her face with ringlets. But I was sure I was right and had found the explanation for a certain strangeness I was becoming aware of in her, for an extra neatness about her dress and for a quality she had to a greater degree than the other girls, a thing you could only call womanliness.

Watching for the night-twinkle of her eyes behind the warmth of the hair she pulled about her face, I came to a resolve. From time to time it was the fashion for us lads to allow a let-up of the customary scorn of girls and pick one out as a sweetheart. For a week or two the chosen one was allowed to follow her man about, to carry his schoolbag for him and to help count his marble winnings. In return he gave her a share of any good thing he had knocked off and also a kiss or two in the dark now and then. Thus we made in our small world what we thought was a facsimile of our parents' relationship. And it was to this role I had decided to promote the suddenly-

93

grown-lovely Yvonne. Incidentally, such a manoeuvre quite defeated the teacher's idea that he was punishing me by putting me among the girls.

It happened as I wished, though I cannot recollect the stages by which we arrived at sweethearthood. There must have been hold-ups, because of Yvonne's French caution, and because she had a little sister who seemed born to act the part of duenna to us. Little Vera, yes, a suspicious child by nature, much given to appearing silently and unexpected at all the tenser moments and turning a pair of grave and saucer-like eyes upon us. Vera had hardly mastered the art of speech herself, but she always wanted long and complete explanations of anything we said or did. Curiously, her almost continuous presence gave a piquancy to proceedings which necessarily lacked point or goal seeing that we were far too young to concretize the magic of the mood which was now come upon us. Because Vera was around, for instance, I had to make my appointments, offer or ask for endearments, only by spelling everything out, thus bamboozling the young. I had to ask for a K.I.S.S. in the P.A.S.S.A.G.E. because it wasn't safe to say just that. But then the smart little Vera learnt what these letters stood for. We had to invent codes, so that for a while P.E.N. meant 'kiss' and D.O.O.R.M.A.T. stood for 'passage' and then we had to change again. Yvonne loved this concealed daring, so did I often, for it was an echo of the normal adult conspiracy to keep important matters from the young. It made us feel truly linked and, after a fashion, married.

The high spots of this innocent romance came on the Saturday nights. Then her parents went out for the evening. The usual way for parents' outings to be managed in our district was for the eldest child to be bribed to 'mind the house' and to collect for the purpose the assistance of friends. Yvonne called in me as the 'friend'. It must have surprised her parents that she chose a boy to keep her company—I don't know. I do not at all remember them. They dished out a few coppers for the bribe and departed. I went off to buy the sweets and the lemonade—but not at any of our own corner shops. Perhaps I thought this an especially important occasion, or perhaps I was too excited and unnerved to want to meet the comments of the corner, anyway, I used to travel on to a shop which was bright and chilly with its modern-style glass showcases and remote shelves and which did not normally appeal to us because it left so little chance to anybody to fill their pockets while the shopkeeper's back was turned.

When I got back the parents had gone. It was Yvonne's house I came to, Yvonne's and mine. Also Vera's. We shared out the sweets into three equal lots, began our first sip of the lemonade, if it was lemonade, more likely it would be lime juice and soda, or sarsaparilla, or dandelion stout. We were now beautifully alone in this tiny upstairs flat. Yvonne and I became very aware of one another, fat little Vera exceedingly alert to intercept any meaningful glance between us or to understand any words that she shouldn't. The official pastimes for such an evening were looking at postcards, colouring-in or tracing pictures and playing games of snakes-and-ladders. Whatever we chose to do was duly set out on the hearth-rug before a fire Mrs. Daubigny built up last thing on leaving. We could hear the fluffing of small flames breaking through the slack, the shift and crumble of cinders, as we played; and the sense of solitary intimacy grew upon us. Often I was impelled to brave Vera's vigilance with a look which sought Yvonne's eyes and tried to convey to her the wordless emotion I felt. But for a while her glances were quick and bright in the fire-glow, putting me away. Her neat hands fluttered over the hearth-rug or flew to her falling ringlets and you could see she wore the secret ring I gave her, which was to be put on only when we were alone because it was red gold (well, copper), like a wedding ring and hardly suitable for little girls. Yes, she was my sweetheart, true enough.

Presently, when I looked again, her eyes took my glance, deepened to it—'Hi, you,' says Vera, warning-like. But Yvonne was looking towards the door now. 'Was that a knock?' She got up and went out on the landing to listen. There was no knock, of course there wasn't. 'Can you hear, Will?' she called. I hurried out to my cue. In the half-dark at the head of the stairs, which went down and were lost below a fanlight vaguely luminous from a street-lamp, we huddled and hurriedly kissed. Vera didn't dare follow us into the dread stair-darkness, but she suspected a manoeuvre. 'There isn't anybody knocking, I know,' she'd call. 'You're kissing, you are. And I'll tell me Da, I will.' We came back, not sheepishly, for Yvonne would mother and fuss over her sister, and I felt strong and full of masculine pride. We were adult for the time being, tolerant and responsible for this child we were looking after.

It was our charge to see that Vera was put to bed at the right time. Her mother had plaited her hair and seen her into her nightdress before she left. After an hour, the little girl turned sleepy and petulant. Then Yvonne led her to the little bedroom, tucked her in bed and put what remained of her sweets under the pillow. She wasn't going to sleep, though, not her; she'd be listening to all we did, she always warned us. In fact, she did call out once or twice, then no more.

Yvonne and I were free now, but there was no advantage

in this. The sensation of being adult which the presence of the baby sister encouraged in us disappeared with her going: we were children again, playing snakes-and-ladders like mad, and each determined to win. It was only if her parents were unusually late that we again became aware of our companionship in the quiet house. We drew closer in to the fire, she sitting on the fender with pinafore outspread, myself dour and flushed on the hassock, the hot glow from the Aladdin's cave that fire had become heavy on our cheek-bones, and we talked. We talked queerly, I believe, of a never-never aftertime when somehow it was to come about that we lived together on the other side of a great forest, Argonne, Ardennes? It was not purposive talk, not question-and-answer, a curious hypnotic drift of words which produced images on our imaginations that must have resembled the drawings children make at that pre-conscious age. We remembered no detail of it afterwards, but only that we had experienced the strange excitement of a shared dream.

The return of the parents brought our evening abruptly to an end. A feeling of guilt always came upon me then, though I could not be accused of any crime save the general unnaturalness of choosing to spend an evening in girls' company. I was glad to speed away with the briefest and gruffest of 'so-longs' to my late dream-partner, and to hurry past the corner-end to my own door, whatever might hide behind that to seal, or to ruin, the last hour before my own late bed-time.

The association with Yvonne must have died of its own impracticality, I think, or out of the thrust of our separate growths; anyway, if it hadn't, it must have been brought to an end by one of those shiftings which so frequently broke off our friendship. Yvonne's family suddenly moved from the Avenues. At that time, families were always moving. There were houses to let everywhere. People believed in houses as the best investment for a bit of cash. You could see where your money was, if you owned a house; it was safe, safe as houses, the very phrase, and you couldn't say safer than that unless you brought in the Bank of England which was too big altogether for the local men and their well-warmed nest-eggs. Builders kept putting them up in response to a demand which seems now oddly lop-sided. It was so largely a demand from landlords, would-be, not from would-be tenants. On the tenants' part there was a fairly common objection to paying rent, evictions and moonlight flits were always going on somewhere in the Avenues, and many of the women were as fond of taking a new house as they were of buying a new hat. After all, it cost nothing, or next to nothing. Most of the moves were across two or three streets. You hired a barrow for threepence;

your old man and the bloke from next door did the shifting;
you gave them a shilling out of your purse so they could get
a few pints to lay the dust with; and you could start life anew.
My pal, Wilf Rowley, departed like that one wet Saturday
morning, so had Freddy Tingall. I never noticed Yvonne go,
because I didn't stand to get any discarded junk from her as I
did from the boys, but go she must have done. Perhaps she was
the last of these disappearances. Then that era of mobile
domesticity ended, and has not since been resumed—the
1914–18 war was upon us.

The corner-lads welcomed it, of course. We thrilled to the
prospect of great British victories, new Trafalgars and
Waterloos, and if the cost was a few fathers killed, well, we
reckoned we could stand that. There was even a certain
amount of eagerness to see fathers march off to glory leaving
us as the only man in the house. We saw ourselves grabbing
the best chair as by right, getting first cut off the joint, smoking
publicly and unrebuked at our own firesides. As plotted out
at the corner-end, war seemed to be just the thing that boys
had always needed. But I had a feeling deep-down that war
wouldn't apply somehow to my father. I couldn't see him
waving a flag and leaping over a parapet, as the wild bugles
blew, straight into the enemies' fire; I *could* see him sitting
firmly as ever in his own chair, pointing out that the war was
a lot of fat-headedness started by old grannies and bosses-on-
the-make and carried on by young fools who believed what
they said in the newspapers.

The realistic view was soon proved right. In the general
agitation of the first few weeks, we got a more-than-average
beat-up of uncles at our place. After the customary visit to
the boozer, argument waged hot and strong. Uncle George,
Boer-war veteran, would join up at once—only there was no
one to run his greengrocery business if he did. True-blue
Uncle Will was hot against the Germans; he would throw in a
couple of sons against them right away—the sons, though, did
not endorse this generous patriotism. Red Uncle Robin,
bachelor, vegetarian and crank, saw the conflict as a power-
struggle between rival groups of bosses to be boycotted by all
intelligent working-men. Sad Uncle Andrew thought it was
one of those madnesses good men have to go in to because
they couldn't stand being among the crooks and sharpers
who'd stay out. Burly, gentle Uncle Bill knew no rights or
wrongs in it, he had the countryman's view, that it was a super-
thunderstorm or tremendously bad weather—'Thor's ne help
for it, we'll hae t'last it oot.' As was his way, my father opposed
each view in turn, and I, hanging around the outskirts of the
group as they stood outside the pub or around our doorstep

or in our kitchen, big strong men dressed in the workers' civvies of the Sunday suit and with the marks of their various crafts upon them, I got his drift by counting up the number of bulls he scored. Like this. To the Brave Little Belgium gambit, he replied that the Belgians weren't as brave as the Germans otherwise they'd have beaten them, and if they hadn't made a mess of things in the Congo they could have had enough black troops to equal the enemy strength, anyway. How would he like being under German rule? Why, the German railway union was quite as strong as the N.U.R., and their conditions were rather better—he'd belong to that. Would he stand by if a German soldier was about to rape his wife? He wouldn't; he'd break the bloke's neck; but he wasn't going all the way to France to find the fellow that might be planning the rape, not likely. Wouldn't he fight for his freedom as a Briton? As a Briton, he didn't have any; he was a British wage-slave, and what freedom he had he'd fought for through the trades union movement; he'd continue to fight for it whether the railway company was owned by Englishmen, Jews, Germans or Scots. Now all these cracks came out in the thrust of argument. You couldn't be sure that what my father argued was what he absolutely believed. All the same, the early hopes both my mother and I entertained of having a hero in the house quickly faded. It wasn't long before we were glad of his decision, seeing so many families desolate and limping. Of course, nobody who knew him questioned his courage: he was 'arkward', that's all. Where he wasn't known, out on the main streets, pretty girls presented him with white feathers, and often—after he'd kidded them a bit and they'd had a good look at him—with their addresses. So he didn't do too badly out of that. A good political conscience is an excellent foundation for adultery.

Chapter Ten

CORNED-BEEF CRIME

The majority of the men round were not of my father's opinion. They rushed to the colours in such numbers that the War Office didn't know where to put them. One Saturday morning a rumour came round that the schools were to be commandeered as temporary barracks; a second report said that the soldiers were already in. Some of us tore round to have a look. Chillingham Road School stood bare and empty, a maw gaping for Monday. We back-pedalled round a corner so as to put it out of sight again, wishing we hadn't come. But somebody passing on a bike said that North Heaton was taken. We moved off into the territory presided over by that semicissy academy, hunching together in case we got raided on the way.

It was true. North Heaton School echoed to the bawls of a couple of sergeants drilling their awkward squads in the boys' yard; every window held the grinning faces of the recruits; there was a coming and going of khaki at the gates; and North Heaton kids lined the railways as they begged for buttons and badges. Lucky North Heaton! we thought: it might so easily have been us. Then one of their lads, who used to be at our school till his family moved, brought us better tidings. We were to go on half-time, sharing our school buildings with North Heaton, we having the morning session, they the afternoon, and vice-versa week and week about.

Well, that was fine. We welcomed North Heaton to our class-rooms and precincts, and didn't mind the alien scrawls they left on our desks and doors. It was such a relief to walk out a free man at twelve that first week and to know that on the next we could lie peacefully in bed mornings asking not for whom the bell tolled, it was not for us. And if we enjoyed the relaxation, it probably saved our young teacher from the gas-oven or the river, which alternatives he must have been considering after each tough session with us.

But then, misplaced zeal and excessive ingenuity got to work. It was decided to give us huge amounts of homework to make up for what we were missing. For what we were missing! Dismay spread through two schools. There was only one thing in the world that was more utterly dislikeable than

99

lessons and that was homework. Even our parents didn't like us doing it, and that shows you. We had some hopes that it might be dropped altogether in war-time, now it was to be doubled, trebled, what have you? Oh, impossible, we over-exploited lesson-slaves wouldn't stand for it. We'd call a strike. Strikes, by the way, were not unknown at our kind of school, we being our fathers' sons and having natural strike-sympathizers in them. Well, this was a striking matter, we thought. It didn't prove so. We got as far as making lists of volunteers for picket-duty and holding conference with the North Heaton leaders, but the whole thing was half-hearted somehow. A single attempt at picketing petered out. The times were not with us.

To my own riotous class, anyway, the grievance was a theoretical one. Every morning we showed up with no home-work done, none at all. This was due, so we declared to a man, to the fact that we'd had sick headaches, all of us. And all our mothers were too busy to write the customary notes, 'excuses', explaining this. Young Mr. Heslop (Hessy for short) gulped and goggled over the mass-afflicted but he had to let it go. In any case, he would never have bothered my desk much. I was back on the boys' side of the room now, sharing a seat with a cross-eyed, cow-licked lad called Warmy, to whom the fairies had given but one talent: he could regurgitate at will. He did and all. Whenever the situation got difficult, he'd gasp out, 'Please, sir, A'm gannin' te——' and begin to retch. He wasn't kidding either. An obstinate and disbelieving teacher got the lot over his boots and trousers as the upheaving Warmy butted blindly into him. Now if I'd any awkward inquiries about homework to deal with, I'd only to give Warmy a nudge, and the little horror obliged at once.

Of course, we were killing our goose. More and more frequently there swept into our uproar the scholarship teacher from next door. A bull-like man, pock-marked and with a habit of irritably scratching at his arse, he was used to quelling his class and keeping them quelled. He had no aversion to giving corporal punishment, and this was very well known indeed. Now we found one sad morning that he was to super-vise our homework, while the wretched Hessy sat withdrawn at his desk pretending to be busy with papers. He'd brought his own strap with him, we noticed, and we were prepared to believe that it was specially treated to cause the maximum pain or at any rate stiff with the blood of generations of vic-tims. The sick headache excuse was no excuse to him. Most of us prepared to plead guilty and take a belting. That seemed to suit him too, probably because it was quicker and he wanted to get back to his own class, the little scholarship marvels

100

who were quiet as mice even in his absence. Up and down the aisles, boy after boy stepped out of his desk, the strap flailed, and boy after boy sat down again hugging his aching palms. It came to us anon. Poor old Warmy for the first time in a life of public service couldn't be sick. He felt sick, I dare say, he looked sick but he couldn't be. He was belted first and ordered off to the lavatory afterwards, ignominiously. I took mine next, rather badly because I under-estimated the teacher's swing and got the first one too high up the wrist where it would leave a weal. Altogether, you might say, a poorish morning and worse to come: later that day, it was plain, we should have to do homework.

Not long after that Warmy disappeared, nobody knew how or why. He was never really popular, except in an emergency, and his fame was not endearing. Next to me now was a vacant place. That is why I was particularly interested in a newcomer who was brought in one morning after Scripture. A tall, slight, wiry lad, with a bone-pale skin and ginger hair, alert like a runner and easy in his self-possession—he'd do, I thought. As expected, he took the place next to me. In no time we seemed well known to each other. During that day I did the honours of our humble round, such as they were, and at the end of it we were fast friends.

Charley Dodd came from Elswick over the other side of the town. His father died about a year earlier, leaving three boys for his widow to bring up. Charley, the eldest of them, was given to looking after his rather pretty mother, was something of a courtier to her when they went out shopping together. You could see his lithe dancer's walk was well paced to take a woman on his arm; and he had the intelligence and the sympathy to share her interests while keeping the best of himself aloof from them. This intelligence of his was a godsend to me and he must have found some similar quality in my own make-up for we had a mutual enhancement in each other's company. For the next two years we kept making the running for each other, though we never became fatally competitive, each knew what the other knew, and there were none of our contemporaries to equal us.

Don't think from me saying that, that we were a pair of solitaries. It was rare, in fact, for us to be on our own. Not long after our first encounter we were busy launching the first of a series of super-gangs intended to be a nobler and more closely-knit organization than you were likely to get out of the chance association of the corner-end. Perhaps, the original kick-off for this came in Charley's peculiar geographical situation. He was an alien from Elswick who lived on the other side of Chapman Street at the extreme end of

Chillingham Road. We had to fit him in somehow. Furthermore, before he came my chief pals were drawn from Sixth and Eighth, Third having suffered the denudation of removals and scholarships. We needed some non-territorial grouping to mark off us chosen from the mongrel clans about, something picturesque and capable of inspiring unusual loyalty. After a couple of trial attempts, we hit on just the thing.

It was called 'The Sons of the Battle-axe'. I was perpetual President, or High Chieftain; Charley, my permanent Vice; and our followers numbered some four or five of the faithful, and another three or four floaters. On joining, you signed the Oath of Allegiance, read the rules and promised to pay one penny a week. You were then given a card, the size of a visiting-card, which had on one side a crude drawing of a battle-axe crossed with a claymore and on the other, your number. You could then be admitted to the Grand Lodge, the Witanagemot, in short, to my bedroom. This was lit by a varying number of shipyard candles, pink to indicate that they contained rat poison, and by a single paraffin bull's-eye lantern which stood on the table with its glass turned to red to show that we were in session. There wasn't much space in that narrow back bedroom so it was just as well that our active membership was not large and the muster any one night rarely exceeded five or six. They began to turn up just as I was finishing my tea. The first couple stuck their heads in the passage and whistled the old tune 'Your pals are calling, there's a knock at the door'. As I went into the bedroom to prepare for them, a glance along the passage showed two black shapes against the violet dusk in the coloured glass panes of the inner door. I lit a candle, removed an ewer full of piss which stood at the foot of the bed to do duty as a chamber-pot, and hurried along the passage to let the boys in. There would be subsequent arrivals and when we judged that all likely to come, had, then we pulled out a long table by the bedside and lit the bull's-eye lantern. Now three could sit on the bed, two on chairs opposite, and one each head and tail of the table. The lantern was turned to red; the secret affairs of the Sacred Battle-axe could now be discussed.

Now and then my sisters would seize a chance to peep in. Once my father did. What they saw, though furtive, was harmless enough. A table-full of conspirators bent round the red eye, above their heads in the glasses of many pictures the reflected flames from the pink shipyard-candles leapt and shuddered to a perpetual draught from the open window behind. That window was let down from the top in order to cover up a shattered bottom pane which had never been re-

102

placed. It was a kind of reason which operated in the household but of course, the neighbours didn't believe it; they thought Mrs. Kiddar's boy had got T.B.—oh, that poor, unlucky woman. Anyway we had the naked sky looking in on us. It made the fire all the brighter, if we had a fire. That depended on the state of stocks in our coal-house, or whether we could be bothered to organize a raid on somebody else's. Even if no fire, the space above the fireplace still flaunted the regalia of our Order. Against a background of the draped Royal Standard, there hung from a deer's head made of chalk (which I won at the hoop-la), a shield bearing the coat-of-arms of the Sons of the Battle-axe, arrived at after much consultation of authorities and guaranteed now, so Charley and I would bet, to satisfy the whole College of Heralds; and on the mantelpiece itself, a cut-glass salt-cellar and mustard-pot flanked by two porcelain coronation chairs, this lot having been stolen from a china-shop in the town.

The character of these meetings was frequently modified according to what we had been reading recently, or what films we'd seen. There was a period when we addressed each other formally by our Indian names. I was Gimo-gash (whose words were wisdom); Charley was White Eagle; Freddy, the swift-footed, was Running Deer; and so on. We took these names from the handbook of the Woodcraft Indians of America, an organization which provided us with a lot of ammunition in our rivalry with the local boy scouts and boys' brigade. We scorned these both, because they were run by adults and ribbon tied with cissy recommendations about not smoking and being a good boy in the home; and we took pains to know all their stuff and a bit more, so that they couldn't claim to have anything on us. They were little cowboys that hadn't come off; we had the real Red Indian sureness, and we walked alone. Says we, of course. The Indian mode gave dignity to our more or less secret smoking, especially if we had no proper fags and were passing round cinnamon shoots bought at the chemist's.

At other times we were Norsemen, the last company of Vikings in history, surviving in the sign of our Battle-axe. And then we were international crooks operating on behalf of some good cause that we never got round to defining. In one guise or another we planned a great many exploits that never came off, and a few that did. The noblest of these, if you count the work it demanded, was our magazine. For some weeks one spring we regularly produced a hand-written paper of eight to twelve pages, which was jellygraphed on a Blick copier and sold at a ha'penny a copy. It went well for a bit. Scurrilous attacks on school-teachers, parodies of school

103

poems, mock warnings of raids on unpopular shop-keepers were the items that sold us. But it was the supply of those, of course, that ran out first. The editors and principal contributors (who were the same identical Charley and me as always was) were getting bogged down in serial and short story; myself in an imitation of Frank Richards which was demonstrating to me, as similar exercises have to so many others, that the old multi-genius is not imitable; and Charley in a Ballantyne opus getting more and more like a series of compositions for the geography lesson punctuated by stray rifle-shots with every issue. The others of our gang contributed some reasonably good drawings, and not-so-good attempts at humour. Outside of our intimate circle there was help coming in large dollops, we always heard. But it always turned out to be the same material as we were stuck on, only much worse. And every rejected contributor was a lost subscriber. There were no volunteers at all for the labour of handwriting, though many wanted to work the copier for us. Things were getting very sticky indeed when we acquired a first-rate excuse for stopping publication. The teachers had seen a copy or two and were prepared to help us. Well, at that we drew ourselves up in noble scorn and considerable relief to give the order: stop the presses.

Most of the time we were not so strenuously engaged. We would quietly forget the opening ceremony and simply sat around talking while a big pan of peas cooked on the fire or potatoes roasted in its ashes. Whenever a fair was imminent, we called all such 'the hoppings', we went into training for it. An improvised board of the 'twenty-five or over wins a prize' variety hung on the bedroom door; a small selection of hoopla objects on the floor awaited our improvised hoops. This practice never yielded all the dividends we promised ourselves, but it certainly saved us from dead loss. From some forgotten source I had acquired an ancient set of boxing gloves. Many a night the walls shook and all the pictures rattled to the thump of bodies. For one of our lads, who was unfortunate in having a withered leg and could only stand on crutches, we had to introduce a new and very non-Queensberry rule: both boxers in this bout had to fight sitting on the bed, to rise on two feet was to lose the round. This innovation never caught on outside our circle, so if we were the material of future champs we couldn't afterwards find the right ring in which to demonstrate our skill. Nobody cared to promote contests between bed-bound and semi-recumbent prize-fighters, we found.

Our enthusiasms were kindled or quenched often enough by the accident of possession. It was the devil's own job for us to get hold of any equipment that cost more than a few coppers. We were likely to hunger a very long time for anything we needed before chance threw something like it our way. For instance, we were regular cinema-goers and also ex-magic-lantern manipulators; each of us had spent long periods at shop windows looking at home cinematographs so impossibly expensive you could only dream of ever owning one. Well, long-continued desire is apt to produce not its true object, but an approximation of it. One day I found myself embarked on a mighty feat of barter which in the end denuded me of my best cigarette-card sets and a ball-bearing skate, but enthroned me in the possession of a workable cinematograph projector of a sort. It wasn't any great shakes, really: a tin cabinet bearing a curved chimney and holding an oil-lamp and its glass; then a gate and handle standing separate, which carried a barely-adjustable lens. With this illumination, the throw was limited to five feet. All the same, it was pretty terrific, we thought; and it would have been very much better if we'd had more films to show. The machine could take ordinary 35-mm. stuff, and what we had were mainly bits and snippets from news-reels. One of the big lads from our corner, actually, he was smaller than me by a lump all round, but as he was working, he rated as 'big,' had a job with Pathé, delivering news-reels on a tricycle, I think. Tich didn't get the sort of salary later current in the world of films, in fact he was often hard put to it to keep himself in Woodbines. He was one of that great tribe of Briton who considered life a fair thing as long as the supply of Woods didn't run out, and when it did would have parted with his grandmother and his only shirt so as to see once again the lovely white cylinder alight in his lips. When we were able to knock off some Woods, we used to waylay him as he came home from work to get lengths of film in exchange.

Thus we built up a collection of snippets. The best was a sequence from an Italian film showing a fire at sea. What made it so good was that it was in colour—not Technicolor, then still a belly-ache in the womb of time, but some kind of dye. It showed a bluish, moonlit sea, across which crept a two-masted schooner (probably a model, but the loyalty to the Battle-axe still latent in me continues to protest that it was genuine). The ship looked so ghostly against the ambience of blue as it bore upon the dark waves you felt that it was doomed, it and the crew we never saw since we were without benefit of close-up still, and sure enough the sign of calamity came upon it. There was a sudden puff of smoke amidships. 'Fire!' said a caption on a blue background, as I turned the handle faster because we all knew that. 'Fire at Sea!' said a

105

caption on a red background, and I slowed down ready for the reappearance of the ship now being licked by red flames and a pretty lurid sight, I can tell you. 'Ooh,' said my audience. I turned more and more slowly in order to make it last, which it wouldn't do for long, because that was all we had of that. There was no proper end to it. When last seen that ghost ship still bore its blossom of flame across the hopeless empty seas and left us with that slight after-yearning which is the sign of perfect pleasure.

Well, that was our best piece. Now for our worst. One tremendously wet night I was out buying that week's *Gem* on the windy corner where Geeling, the newsagent's, was. Lord, it was wet. There was such a wind about, too, that you could see the rain coming at you, flung in whole sheets all the way across the Junction, shawls of it, ropes of it, lashing round your legs, clapping down like a watery cloche over your bent head, and flattening in liquid running veils on the lit shop windows. There were few about, you bet. The shops stayed undisturbed behind the wet gaslight they showed outside. Even the fish-and-chip was so blinded and sealed up in this flat rain, you couldn't taste a smell from it. But in the dark doorway next to it, there stood a small figure who gave me a hail. I swung the peak of my dripping cap around. It was Tich, the big lad from Pathés. He was broke and hungry; he wanted some chips. What's more, he had on him the biggest roll of film I'd yet encountered—oh, there must have been two hundred feet of it. Of course, I'd only the penny for my *Gem*, but there wasn't going to be anybody else about on such a night—Tich reckoned it would have to be a deal.

So it was, indeed, but what a disappointment. The whole film showed nothing but a visit of the King and Queen to a Tyneside shipyard. At least that is what a caption said. You see, it is a well-known fact that whenever any distinguished visitors are due on the Tyne, you reach for your mack; if they are going to a shipyard, reach for two macks because if there is any place wetter than a shipyard on a rainy day, it must be in Davy Jones's province. Not that you could see any rain in this picture; all you could see was a soup-plate, Queen Mary, stalking a saucer, King George. Sometimes other pieces of china strolled across or retreated into the murk, but they were just flashes of pans, you might safely say. Just at the end, a ghostly motor-car wrapped itself round the crockery, and a line of washing waved to it. That was all this immense footage gave one. Whenever I showed it to younger audiences they yelled that my lamp was going out; and they never asked to have it run through again.

One night we got an idea for the salvaging of this wasted

106

footage. Why not scrape the roll free of film and draw cartoons on it. You can imagine what we'd let ourselves in for. It isn't easy to draw on celluloid, less so if you are rationed to the 35-mm. frame for space, and only two of us were any good at drawing anyway. After many hopeless attempts, we hit on a formula. Our characters would be match-stick men, so that any one of us could follow the master-drawing; and their adventures would be limited to what could be done with the simplest of props, a lamp-post, say, or a chamber-pot. This worked, you know. It enabled us to set up a sort of poor boy's Hollywood of doorstep Disneys. We had script and production conferences properly controlled by the general awareness that anybody who thought he had a good idea would presently have to make it. A wearisome labour it was, too. Amazing what a perseverance boys will put into a task if nobody has told them to do it. Night after night with homework shelved and forgotten we struggled with spluttering pens over the celluloid coils. The result was a great success with our public. We hit Broadway to some extent when we were invited to put on a show at a rather posh girls' party. After that we dreamed of greater ventures and performed none.

All the winter long we kept fairly well together. It was the coming of the light nights that made attendance irregular and contributions nil. There were periods when you might have thought our association defunct, and we did ourselves almost. Yet it was remarkable how the members returned to us when we needed to organize a stunt. For instance, it was reported early one evening that a butcher's back window was broken. The report was not made with any intent or purpose; we were not in session, just idling about vaulting the iron posts at the top of Fourth and arguing about the best kind of tent to buy when we were well enough off to buy one. So the news of the butcher's window at first merely provoked humorous cracks about the cats of the neighbourhood helping themselves. One after another we continued to spit on our hands and haul ourselves with a hop over each of the four posts and back into the conversation again.

But then it occurred to someone to remember that at times we were a gang of international crooks. We missed nothing, not us. Our spy-ring was always on the look-out weighing up banks and bullion-trains, ready to spot any weak link in the chain of safeguards which our intrepid and keen-eyed master-crooks could instantly take advantage of. Here we had one of our spies returned to us with his report. We would make use of it, sure : we'd produce a plan. Right. Our best draughtsman got out pencil and paper. Now for the facts. The butcher would be shut now, and as it was a lock-up shop there could be no interference from him. But next door, the old lady or her daughter might have wandered out of the sweet-shop into the yard, and hear our movements. We must set some one of us the task of creating a diversion in the shop. Now for the assault on the back premises. At this point we found the original report lacking in detail: it was decided that we should have a more up-to-the-minute survey, and this had better be made by one of Eighth since the back lane we'd need to use was their territory and he could hang about it more legitimate-like.

He went. He came back. Like all subordinates in crime out-fits, he'd shown too much zeal: he'd actually climbed over into the butcher's backyard, and might have blown the plot prematurely. But as zeal always does in crime stories, it had repaid him: he could now report that behind the broken window were bars. We couldn't get in. I think we were all relieved at this. We didn't really want to risk being caught on the premises, especially not on such unpromising premises as a butcher's, to be caught red-handed with a lump of liver or a fistful of cold tripe seemed a bit inglorious. A wave of let's-drop-it went blowing round the company. Our spy had another bit of news yet to add: behind the bars were a number of large tins of corned beef. The dream of large dollops of corned beef glowed upon the countenance of the assembled ever-hungry. Besides, for our credit's sake we had to make at least a pass at the project. One of us had a knife with a screw-driver attachment. Right, then boldly the others deputed him to force the bars knowing damn well he'd never succeed if you gave him all night to do it. That agreed, on paper, we worked out a division of forces: one to keep guard at each end of the lane; one to create a diversion in the sweet-shop; one to stand opposite the butcher's back-door and give the wire if anything went wrong inside; and two to carry out the actual crime (still undefined largely). Got it, boys? Then we're off.

All our plans got the go-by right from the start. Where the butcher's was, Eighth Avenue lane debouched; and when we arrived it was in the fullest and liveliest occupation by a crowd of small fry busy stoning a cat, or coaling it rather, coal being the most plentiful missile round those parts. They had tied a can on to the cat's tail expecting it to behave as a dog would when similarly equipped. But this was an alley-cat. It didn't move a couple of yards before it hauled itself up on a coal-house roof and now sat there swearing and biting with its teeth at the string on its tail. It isn't easy to tie anything on a cat's tail that will stay put for any length of time, and soon after our arrival, the rattle of the tin down the tiles of the roof announced that the cat was free. Now all these lesser folk turned on us, wanting to sponge sweets if we had any, fag-ends, cigarette-cards, anything. They wanted to keep up their excitement and very nearly anything would serve their turn. As we stood glum, the cheeky ones were already pretending to spit on our boots and starting to call our names. They drew us out; we had to chase them off, for there was simply no ignoring them.

But one of us must have managed to slip away without being noticed. We didn't miss him ourselves at first. When we did, it dawned on us where he must be. We would have to shake off these kids. We moved off in a body towards the Seventh Avenue sweet-shop, all the tribe dancing around us like flies about a horse. At the shop we separated and walked quickly away in opposite directions. The small fry decided we must have no money and began a drift back to their own street.

We met again on the quiet Ninth where we guessed our fellow-criminal would be. He was there sure enough, being over-furtive and highly-excited at the same time as he clutched to him a bulky object wrapped in a bit of sacking. His story, quickly told, was that he dropped over the yard-wall, crept along bent double to the window to see if there was any hope of shifting the bars, and though there wasn't, for they were firm enough, they were not evenly spaced. He put his hand through the widest space where the last bar came and found he could touch a corned-beef tin, wangle it forward, and it might just clear the bar. With some wangling, out it came; he picked up a bit of sacking and fled with it.

We looked on him with some admiration, not absolutely undilute, as he whispered his tale. The point now was, where should we take this thing under the sack? It was a sum-mer evening with everyone on the streets, remember. No, I did not suggest using our headquarters, and neither did any-one else. This huge tin—it seemed to be getting bigger all the time—was both conspicuous and quite inexcusable. What about the pictures? There was enough money in the circle for three of us to go—at that the other three said with a suspiciously-hasty optimism that they'd go home, get their money and join us on the way. Don't wait, they'd catch us up. Before the rump could think of another alternative, they were gone. So the two of us left saw nothing for it but to line up with the culprit and begin a cruelly-casual stroll to the Scala, he hugging his red-hot white elephant of a corned-beef can, we avoiding all mention of it. What made things awkward after a bit was that this late daring criminal would keep say-ing that he didn't see why he should do all the loot-carrying as well as the lifting. We spent as much time as we could explaining that the whole glory of the thing was his, but he finally revolted and threatened to dump his cargo on the pavement. After that we took turns—it was damned heavy, too, give him that.

The reason why it was heavy was that there was a lot in it. Was there not! Our idea had been that we were going to finish it off in the pictures; so far in a hard life we'd never had any reason to doubt the capacity of our appetites. Well, would you believe it, that cornucopia of corned beef just wouldn't get finished. Great chunks kept coming along the row whenever the screen darkened, lovely grub, mind you, lovely grub, but getting greasier and more blotting-papery under the taste with every round. There was no doubt about it we were getting full. We were getting beefed up to the neck, we were as glassy-eyed as the dead bull we hadn't yet devoured, not all, our fingers were becoming hateful to us. 'Is it nearly finished?' we whispered to the holder of the can. 'Na, plenty here yet.' Pause, sigh, chew on. No doubt another round would have come up if one of us hadn't found the resolve to say suddenly, 'Put it under the seat, eh?'

Ah-h! We now turned our bovine attention to the screen. It couldn't have been a thrilling film—I, for one, was willing to dash out before the end and before the lights went up, leaving our tin under the seat. Presently, however, the corned-beef-crammed cranium cleared a little. We were sitting in our usual seats; when that can was found under them, who among the patrons could be suspected of taking such unusual and outsize refreshment to the cinema? The answer was clear—us!

I whispered these cogitations to my pals right and left. Right pal thought, perhaps we could eat the rest. Silence. Left pal considered we'd better chance taking it with us in the rush.

That is why for this night only we came home from the Scala via First Avenue, which would be absurd except that First Avenue faces the trees and allotments lining the railway embankment—here there should have been a good hiding-place.

There wasn't. By next day, a Saturday, we were all in good fettle again. We planned to spend the afternoon at a spot known to us, and to us only, as Gore, Blood and Guts Gulch, but which was actually the harmless, over-grown slag-heaps standing around the long-abandoned shaft of an old pit. For this we intended laying in our usual stock of lemonade, stale cakes, bruised fruit, and broken biscuits. The corned beef was to be the welcome stranger at our usual feast. But it was gone! The three who weren't at the planting of it, and who by now were ashamed of their last night's retreat and ex-

110

ceedingly lecherous of canned meat foreby, suspected that one of the three who were there had pinched it. But we of the sated three had no such thought. Not one of us was capable of a second corned-beef crime, once had proved so very amply enough. Perhaps we'd been followed by some alien from another corner? If so, we'd hear of it presently, since their crowd were bound to boast of scoring off us. Perhaps, one of the railwaymen out of the side bar of the Chillingham had spotted our movements and come over to see what we'd been doing. Happy in his beers he'd think it a good thing likely enough to dish out our meat in the pub. We lay on the top of the biggest slag-heap debating these alternatives, and some less probable others. Three of us were not much bothered in any case: we'd had the danger and the glory and the fat reward; now all was over, we hoped, and we could stretch out peaceably on this high place looking out on aerial acres tremulous with lark-song towards the distant big wheel of the Wallsend pit which was immobilized, of course, in its Saturday stillness. Presently, perhaps after we'd eaten our cheap shop-scourings, the gang of international crooks would dissolve into another of its manifestations. This summer sky we looked on now owed its eastern glory, we believed, that is the clear blue and salt crystalline sparkle which was never seen in our industrial west and south, to the fact that there it bent to the sea. Well, we were a sworn band of explorers pledged to future exploit—let's go to the coast.

There were ways of doing that, and ways. The coast was only a matter of eight or nine miles away and served by a circuit of fast electric trains. Our families went there regularly through the summer, those with railway associations cheaply by privilege ticket. But that wouldn't do us at all. Whoever heard of an expedition taking an electric train up the Amazon? Or travelling with a lot of women and kids?

We had to proceed on the lines laid down by the best authorities. On the night before, we got out a map, traced out a route with carbon papers so that we had a copy each; marked on each copy significant details to enable us to get our bearings and also the names of places that were slightly unfamiliar to us and might be worth investigation as we passed by. The destination and the place of assembly was written on in cypher and each sheet concealed, when we were feeling extra-ingenious, in a small potato. In that shape, a copy could be handed to any member not then present without anyone about knowing of our plans. Secrecy was essential.

We met one by one, by the barber's opposite our house. As it was so soon after breakfast, it was a quiet morning street we stood in, bare to the open day. The sunburst of the sum-

111

mer dawn was over, of course, the sky already had a great height where it curved over the junction bending to that distant sea and the few cloud-puffs marking it. Despite our precautions anyone who was by, could see that we were on expedition bent, because we each carried a brown paper parcel containing sandwiches or some such. My own principal fare was usually three baked herrings, or some sausage rolls, to make the substantial core to whatever else the pantry might afford in the way of eatables. My earlier pals had to wait while this was being packed and while I tried every persuasion to increase my stock of copper a bit more beyond the bare fares. We could usually count on getting the fare and at least a penny over, all of us; and we always reckoned to save more than half of it by walking all the way there and half back. I don't think we ever bothered to consult our rough route-map once we got started; we knew all the ways of getting to the coast, anyway, so why should we?

When all that were coming by the look of things had arrived and we'd teased any inquisitives that were about with long stories of how far we were going, we drifted off. There were cries of 'They're gannin te the seaside, there, I knew they wor', from whoever had been quizzing us, and a last-minute upstairs-window wail, 'Now divn't ye be late, our Fred, else yor Da will pay ye, he will.' We moved down to the Junction, all the east in our faces and an endless day to come.

Yet the first couple of miles always tried our patience. On our left the dark caverns of a series of engineering works puffed oil-fumes at us; on the right, the destructor chimney occasionally fanned down its foul smoke; even the oncoming air had the rattle of riveting-guns from the shipyards in it; and yet we had the whole length of the river to walk before we were clear of industrialism. So at Wallsend Boundary we were tempted to take a tram. Half-price on a North Shields tram, that was our ticket. Newcastle trams were dearer, and they ended at the Boundary; Tynemouth trams were dearer still but we could walk that last bit from Shields. Walk? We often ran. Why here, from North Shields on, the air was full of the great sea-glow, a salt radiance brightened all the long Tynemouth streets. And at the end of them, the land fell off at the cliff-edge into a great shining nothingness immense all ways over the lazy crimping of seas on their level floor.

Tynemouth has everything a seaside town should have, and what it hasn't, you can get next door at Cullercoats. It has a pier—I mean a real one, not an amusement parade on stilts. Tynemouth pier is a real bastion, huge blocks of sun-tinted granite which hold off the whole weight of the northern seas from the river-mouth. We used to follow the long curve of it

112

to its lighthouse, and stand there looking across to its opposite number, the South Pier, and waiting as long as we could stand the inaction in the hope that a really big ship, a warship best, would come in. Sometimes, one did. Or one left, lifting and ducking like a row-boat no matter how big she was as she passed the harbour-bar. If she was Tyne-built we swelled with communal pride and wished we were on her, going to rule far seas by the might of riveted steel and true craftsmanship.

Tynemouth has the ruins of an ancient priory, and a modern fort; it has high cliffs and long stretches of white sand. Now during the day we were drifting irregularly by these matters, going in the main ever-north. Very likely we stopped to explore caves and rock-pools, to fish with pins and limpets off the breakwater to Cullercoats tiny harbour, to hang about the amusement park in Whitley Bay's Spanish City. Late on, if we were far enough up the Monkseaton sands and the tide was out, we might cross over the rocks to St. Mary's Island where another and more accessible lighthouse stood. But it needed full summer to get all that in and still have daylight in hand when we finished.

One thing was certain. At the end of the day, we'd have spent all we had, including the coppers we meant to save for tram-fare. We had to walk back, therefore, either the way we came or by the northern route through the colliery villages of Backworth and Benton. Whichever way one took, it was too far. For one thing, we always over-estimated our walking speed—do it in two hours easy, we said. So we hung on to the seaside until every sign said it must be pretty late. Even then for the first few miles we were readily diverted and delayed by objects of interest on the way. Then at last our wonderful summer sky began to fail us. Its remote spun-blue and the fine etheric sparkle dimmed to an opaque forget-me-not; its ceiling quietly lowered. Distant trees that had been standing all day under sun-showers and seemed permanently fused with light, became black and stood a step nearer every time we looked at them. For long stretches we were silent, our eyes often studying the gutters in the hope that somebody had dropped a purse, or even a single salvaging shilling to give us a tram-ride over the last two miles from Benton. We never found a purse; what shillings that appeared always turned out on closer examination to be silver paper or a recently laid gobbet of spit. Stiff-legged, weary, hunger a great hole in us, we dragged the last couple of miles through the unedifying dusk.

Chapter Eleven

THE 'MA GANG' THEIR OWN POLTERGEISTS

Some of our expeditions were more ambitious than that, further afield and to stranger places, but our range was always limited by the fact that none of us owned a bicycle, and our pocket-money over these years was (officially) no more than one to three pennies a week. True, it was supplemented by our own earnings. From a very early age, we ran errands (called 'messages') for all and sundry. You had to train your memory for this job since not every customer would be bothered to write out a list, even if she could write. One tongue-twister that nearly had me beat was an order for 'tincture of lobelia and syrup of tolu'. I had to take the coppers out of my mouth so as to gabble that line as I ran at full speed to the chemist's. If there were two or three in the shop, I had to stand there saying 'tincture of lobelia and syrup of tolu' over and over again under my breath, incessantly. Leave off a moment, start reading labels on bottles or merely pause to inhale the incredible mixture of smells which is the chemist's own climate, and you'd lost it.

As we grew older, each of us had built up a Saturday morning round of 'messages', and could count on a poorish return of odd ha'pennies, slices of Dutch cheese, buns or apples. Or you might get the job of scrubbing out someone's backyard for a penny. Similarly, a little girl could hearthstone a doorstep or polish the brasses. There was the steady bottle-trade, too: any boy sent to get beer from the off-licence got the ha'penny on the empty. When I reached the ripe age of twelve, however, my first real job came along. A schoolmate of mine, not much older, worked every Saturday afternoon at the Singer Sewing Machine shop in Grainger Street, pushing a barrow loaded with machines down to the station parcels office. They wanted another lad, says he. The pay was one shilling, and the job proved to be ideal. I was shown a cellarful of obsolete sewing-machine stands, given a coal-hammer, and told to smash them up. Well, what would you think? I waded into all that cast-iron junk with such energy that I found myself out of work three Saturdays later.

From a newspaper round which I started on one wet even-

114

ing I discharged myself automatically by being quite unable to rise in time for the morning delivery. A peach of a job followed that: scrubber at a fried fish saloon. When that fizzled in a change of ownership, Charley and I began to work up a really good racket. The war had been going on so long, with deeper and deeper dredgings of the country's stock of men, that labour of all kinds was getting scarce. Round the railway stations, for instance, there was often neither taxis nor porters. We found we could pick up a bit carrying people's bags for them. The first snag we saw in this was that men customers didn't like facing the fair comment of the street if they walked along empty-handed followed by two boys struggling to haul a suitcase between them. If we were reduced to working for women, we didn't get well enough paid. The answer to this was a barrow. Now an old man with a dropped eye who kept goats on a bit of waste ground near the Destructor, offered to lend us one at the all-in price of four-pence a day. The barrow smelled strongly of billy-goat sometimes, but it gave us a professional status. There were days when we did so well, out of sailors on leave and such, that we felt even scandalously rich.

I think that most of our money went on food. It was a time of U-boat warfare, potato queues, closed butchers, dark and puddeny bread, general shortage. Housewives were more than ever at their wits' ends to know how to make do; unsympathetic husbands often blamed the cook; it was exasperating to see some folks' awkward bairns picking round their plates as carefully as though they were matching beads or something. When I tell you, believe it or not, that even growing boys got indigestion, you'll gather that eating was not the delight it has reason to be. Meals caused rows among the most angelic, especially among them. For the 'good', that is those who don't drink, or smoke, or beat their wives, have a terrific lust for grub. They are secret cake-eaters, slippers into pantries out of hours, packers of starch in bulk, pursuers of quaint pick-me-ups consisting of something with jam on. And, of course, they are totally lacking in the elementary sense of shame, remorse, or conscience which guides the normal person's conduct between bouts. So off the handle these offended addicts flew. There were rows where rows didn't ought never to have been, under the texts and within a teacup-throw of the Family Bible—oh, shocking they were.

In our house, however, things domestic had actually bettered in one respect. The demands of the Great War limited our little one by procuring the more frequent absence of one of the contending forces. At this time my father was a spare link man. That needs some explanation. A link is a number

115

of weekly turns, both back-shift and day-shift, worked by the footplate staff engaged in various kinds of railway traffic. Each week, driver, fireman and guard had the same daily starting-time, and next week it changed. In some twelve to eighteen weeks, the list of starting-times was exhausted, this small wheel of fate had completed its revolution; it started all over again. There were many of these wheels controlling the different kinds of traffic and as each had to be learnt, the railwayman spent years in slowly accumulating a Karma which promoted him from one to the other, from minerals to fast goods, from local passengers to expresses and so on. Now when the war broke out my father had been round enough of these wheels and acquired sufficient knowledge of types of engines and the roads they ran on to qualify for what was called the spare link. This consisted of jobs that were a bit out of the ordinary running, excursions, say, or troop trains. Under the stress of war, these extras to time-table so multiplied themselves that drivers were often reduced to the agreed minimum leisure of six hours off. They didn't necessarily spend even this small freedom at home. The period of time-off might occur when they stepped out of the cab at Edinburgh, York, or Doncaster, and on successive days too, because they could be put on to another job at each of these places.

This being the way of it, we saw little of the old man some weeks, and when he did get home, he was liable to dive into bed pretty quickly and to emerge when the caller's knock announced that he had time only for a meal and, perhaps, half an hour's reading by the fire. He read Dickens, very slowly and with an utter appreciation which valued every word. For months the same volume stayed at his side of the fireplace, or was gripped in his pipe-free hand, scrawled across the back was the famous signature writ in gold : Gnarlio Diebrene.

That sounds harmless enough, but the fact is, we were not often truly at ease when he was present. He always had with him, you see, what was known as his 'bad temper'. He might at any time hold up the easy drift of things-going-wrong-about-the-house with a sudden flare of cold rage. Whether he was right or wrong mattered little to us once he'd started; we knew we were in for an episode of extreme discomfort which could do no good at all after it was over. In his absence, we each tried what we could do to keep mother from straying too far off the tracks. At this time, she was developing an extra boldness of misdemeanour. She was not alone in that, far from being so. Perhaps because the war continued to tear away so many fathers from their hearths, mothers everywhere were getting decidedly uppish. Those that were sociable, as mine was, supported each other. She had to have friends and for years now they had been the kind of friends that one was diffident about inviting into the house, pub-acquaintances, women with half-drowned sorrows that were not sufficiently secret, unlucky ladies all. My mother was very good at discovering female misfortune disguised in milk stout or mild-and-bitter; she was pretty sure to pick up a sister-in-sorrow in any place that had 'Saloon' written on it. When she was missing, that was the reason. She was always running these little errands of misery, as you might call them, and had built up an extensive circle. Now that circle was closing in.

My father called them the Ma gang, because they had a habit of always alluding to each other as Ma This and Ma That. He saw the backs of them, chiefly, but that was enough, since they fled the moment he appeared. All right, only now, he didn't appear often enough. And when I did, it was becoming fairly regular to see Ma McGrewin, or Ma Smailes, or Ma Forbes sitting boldly by the fireside—boldly, I say, but not so boldly after I'd come in. For this was the measure of them: I was of my father's sex, bore some resemblance to him (especially when he wasn't there), was to some extent his representative, and these slender facts made them a trifle uneasy, and a bit placatory even to me. For the first few minutes, the knowledge both parties had that did my father's step sound in the passage one would have to fly, affected both our attitudes. Hence the cracks that were regularly made to the effect that I looked so strong and healthy, was a chip off the old block, but then all Ma Kiddar's children were healthy, you could see they were well looked after. This last was one of a repertoire of compliments which one Ma always paid to another, often with a hiccup for emphasis. Behind another Ma's back even they'd say the same. So it became established by reputation round the circle that they might have a bad name with some folks (several wet lips came out of glasses and tightened), we might take a drink now and then (all nodded slightly in gracious acknowledgement, except Ma Smailes if it was her turn to pay), but we never, oh never, neglect our bairns (ah, smack our lips all, got 'em there, we have).

Now it is a curious fact, contrary to the principles of social hygiene, wise planning, family or private morality, that the children of the Mas were extremely healthy, take 'em all round. Ma McGrewin's brood for instance, drew forth pity from passers-by every winter as they appeared in thin dresses to splash barefoot in the slush. Well, they never ailed a thing. Folks with no children said that's because the devil looks after his own. Other mothers couldn't console themselves so easily as they hurried past the lane-end to get something for little

117

Alfie's chest or Doris's bronchitis and were affronted to come across this gutter-swarm of McGrewin's fairly sparkling and ruddy in their manifest misery.

The second great virtue of the Mas, as they saw it, was that they were always ready to help each other. As we cynics saw it, they were always ready to help themselves from each other. They borrowed. They borrowed from anybody as long as anybody would, and when anybody wouldn't, they borrowed from themselves. Not for use, mind you, not to help out in a domestic contingency. No, they borrowed to pawn. Pawning was the economic master-plan behind their conviviality; the excuse for otherwise unlawful occasions; the 'intent' that saved these busy women from many a charge of loitering in the streets that might have been made against them. Naturally it happened as it does in all business undertakings that a lady might find herself short of material in her own warehouse or emporium. The pawnables were all out and she had nothing she could lay her hands on. But, and thank goodness, she was not a lone operator; she had friends; she could pop round to Ma So-and-So's, and be obliged at once. You can see it was a marvellous system with advantages to all.

My mother's membership of this group certainly speeded up the circulation of the household. Every Monday morning she was as busy as a bee. Start a week well, her every gesture seemed to say. There she was, washed, her hair brushed, the authentic air of purpose properly will-brightened upon her —it was a pleasure to look on one so set for disciplined endeavour. What she was doing, though, was assembling her bundle. It probably included her husband's Sunday suit; it might have tablecloths, sheets, blankets, curtains, vases, books, anything capable of slightly-assisted motion. Off she'd go, bundle in one hand, stick in the other, and when you saw her next, Lord knew.

She wasn't on her own in this. Every street in the districts of Byker and Heaton, to go no further than that, was perfectly familiar with this Monday morning procession of bundle-wallahs. The foreigner might think it was washing-day —so it was in many homes, but these were no washer-women. Here they'd come, mostly one by one, the tidied-up survivors of various week-ends, some with black eyes, some just booze-darkened, some perching their bundles on the swollen pods that testified to a few months' membership of the Pudding Club, some too withered for that, some with prams both empty and full, and some furtive over a disguised freight. The procession always included a small boy or so pushing his bundle along on a soap-box. It converged on the same regular points where the arms of the Medici promised succour to the short-of-cash.

Well, this was pleasant, you know, once you'd got used to it and false pride had fallen off. Ma This and Ma That had met again—on legitimate business, too. They drew their supplies and adjourned to the nearest. There now, it was dinner-time before they knew. However, there was cold meat left from Sunday, if they'd managed a joint (they always talked of 'managing a joint' as if that was a terrific financial operation which only their long experience and house-keeping skill could bring about); and if there was time to put the potatoes on, they would. But a woman's only got one pair of hands and she can't be doing everything at once—that's right, Ma Forbes, and A'm sure you do your share, if you never did any more you've done that, see ye the night, ta-ta, take care of yourself, mind.

They met again in the evening, still floating on the pawn-shop money. Not till the next day did they begin to wonder whether it would last till pay-day. On first starting this game, it did; and it was mighty convenient to a housewife to have thrown this silver bridge over the mid-week penury. Come pay-day they joined another procession, the path of the re-deemers this time, and over the week-end all the household gods were back on their pedestals. It was a classical example of the use of credit except for two flaws in it. Suppose the old man happened to want his best suit through the week and didn't think to give Ma sufficient notice of his need. That was going to cause it. In my father's case (he was probably courting at the time) when this happened, there was a terrific explosion, forests of recently-grown goodwill were flattened and family faces blanched whichever direction you looked. The second trouble was that pawnshop money didn't last very well. The good ladies found themselves by Thursday, and soon by Wednesday, obliged to pay a second visit to the door by the Three Brass Balls. A clock went with them, or the sewing-machine, something handy like that. And this extra levy so piled up the redeeming list that there was less and less housekeeping money left in hand. Sunday joints shrank; be-came rabbits; it wasn't possible to pay the whole bread-man, all of the coal, the milk, or even the rent. Never mind, give these household pests something on account, and when your man discovered what was going on and insisted that you must become solvent somewhere then, let the sewing-machine slide, or the vases, or a clock—you could always pay the interest.

Oh, yes, anyone deserving of the name of Ma *always paid the interest*. It was good to see how these bibulous matrons took a wholesome pride in themselves because of that virtue.

119

Nothing was really lost, you see: they could show you the tickets. All the same, it could happen that a lady might have nothing pawnable by her in the drought-stricken mid-week. There'd be a rattle at our back-door. All knew what it was. If father was in, then Ma Kiddar flushed like a winter sunset, dropped her frying-pan and scuttled down the yard at a surprising speed for a cripple—her husband watching her from the window with a sardonic expression suitable to a racing tout who has just spotted that a Derby fancy is lame in all four legs. A back-door colloquy cut to the bone in wardage, and the deal was off. But if he was out, Ma Smailes or someone like her crept over the clear coast and slid into a kitchen chair with a smile so oily you felt she ought to have salted and vinegared it before she offered it round. After the usual gambit of how well the children looked and such a credit, Ma Smailes unloosed a hand from her oxter, took the other out with it, sat it up and began nursing it—now for the tale of woe. Her husband had to go to a funeral, and needed his Sunday clothes—how could she get them out, in the middle of the week and nothing coming in, and the bairns to feed with her last coppers. Or her eldest daughter was having a baby and she'd had to get some sheets out of pawn because the poor girl hadn't been able to get a stitch together, her husband being in clink at the moment just for taking home a box of oranges that the girl happened to fancy, as we all have our fancies when in that condition. There was no actual moral to any of these tales except that they always came to the point where Ma laid her hand down in her lap as though it had dropped off nicely at last, and became more earnest as she pointed out that she didn't like to trouble anyone, and never had ... That was Ma Kiddar's cue. 'A'm sure you wouldn't,' she'd say soothingly. 'Eh, hinny, A've had troubles meself and know what it is.' And so on, we bystanders knowing at that point that something would go out of the house that we'd probably never see again. 'A won't forget you, mind'—Ma Smailes's last words. She forgot.

So did those who borrowed by the front-door. In fact, pledge-swipers could be held off only by the extreme measure of having pawned everything yourself. Mrs. McGrewin was easily tops in this. She had reduced her household to a bareness which even Thoreau himself had never contemplated. 'Simplify!' said the New England philosopher. Well, she had simplified every room pretty near down to the original bare buff. Venetian blinds, being part of the fixtures, hung down in the front with no curtains behind them. There was one double-bed remaining, doubtless in deference to her husband's humble need, for the rest, the children slept on the

120

floor in room's clockless, vase-less, picture-less, and dish-less—they drank out of jam-jars. In this near-nirvana of the necessities peace reigned. McGrewin himself, who was a fitter and not a philosopher, as you might suppose, was a quiet pipe-smoking man who went to work every day in jacket and boiler suit, took a half-pint by himself in the evenings (never with his missus) when he appeared in a bowler hat and a faded blue suit, was peaceable, put-up-able, never had a bad word for nobody—in short a typical Irishman. Perhaps he had the knack of living in a private oblivion and that was a sufficient happiness, but the children were happy, too. And the kids round about, notably my sisters, loved to go to that house. Life was a perpetual picnic there, we gathered; the only house in the street where they could eat properly off the floor and wash all well down out of a real tasty jam-jar. This was another awkward paradox for the dutiful mother of the district to ponder.

Of course Ma McGrewin looked after her brood. You could see her doing it, could hardly miss seeing her because when tiddly she could keep upright only if she ran. She ran. She passed us often, tearing along Third at great speed, large nose to the fore, black bun dancing, fat white calves over laced boots stotting along like lard-bladders, and some beer-scented whirlpools in the air behind her. She was an alcoholic crow returning to the nest, and, no doubt, she had grub of some sort in her bag. And she appeared to be welcome always to her tolerant family. These were entirely girls for a long time, about four of them, then late and much-wanted, a son arrived. Ma was so delighted with him she kept him on the breast for years, and this led to an odd situation in time. The lad was precocious in some ways; he took to smoking at the age of three, and used to delight some spectators with the way he'd spit the nipple out and toddle across to beg a light for his fag-end, or vice versa. Others deplored the shameful spectacle, or tried to. Nobody ever got a really full heart into deploring the McGrewins, they looked so well on what they did.

My mother was soon well fixed in the pawnbroking cycle and had imparted some mobility to the household environment, though she was too handicapped by an 'awkward' husband to reach the McGrewin perfection. We were getting used to her poltergeist activities. Things were there, then they weren't, then they were again. A heavy raincoat which had hung in the passage as long as I remembered, vanished. It might have been stolen years ago for all we knew, but speculation on those lines was halted suddenly: the coat came back. So did some fine weather: it went again. A *History of the Great War* we were getting, volume by volume as the war

121

progressed, twinkled in and out, never all there and never totally missing either. A work-box, some well-known trinkets, a rolled-gold watch-chain, some decanters, all joined in this fugitive existence. We ceased to ask for anything we couldn't immediately lay hands on, and when it happened to be there all the time, my mother was furious at our easy assumption of her guilt. One day, when my father returned from one of his long work-absences to enjoy some time off, he got into his old game of putting all the clocks in order. Now clocks were very much his perquisite; nobody dreamt of touching them either in his presence or absence. There they all were, plain to be seen; and quietly he went from one to the other, oiling, cleaning, winding, all was well in his world. Until he remembered one he didn't usually bother with, the marble Parthenon in the front room. Gone! Clean gone! Well, of course, it was mother's own clock and given to her truly by presentation, but such matters were not likely to weigh with him. When he called me in to look, I expected war to commence. Curiously, he wasn't even slightly vexed. What had struck him was the mad energy the woman could display in order to raise the wind so briefly, because that clock weighed like a ton of lead and was a strong man's burden if it had to be moved any distance. Yet one crippled body walking with a stick had lugged it out and along several streets, and would no doubt lug it all the way back again. For once, I caught my father simply marvelling at the woman.

If only he could have done that more often. But he couldn't. One has to be untouched in order to marvel, to have emerged only briefly from a private oblivion like that old McGrewin had around him. For the true sunny-natured it is possible to be amused at living in a kaleidoscope of household property in which objects appear and disappear at the whim of a pawn-shop poltergeist, but my father was not sunny-natured. On the contrary he had a well-established role which he must have felt impelled to play up to. The hearth-legend said that he was cursed with a permanent bad temper. Perhaps it wasn't as true as all that, but we believed it, and the reigning belief operates, whether right or half-right, equally well. So much that whenever his key was heard in the lock, or the bed creaked to his rising, the atmosphere flattened, something in the air waited for what was to come.

When he came into it, he didn't interpret this general stiffening as fear of his temper, no, he sensed guilt and a general knowingness of what he didn't. He looked around to find what had gone wrong. There could be plenty. Mother had, perhaps, only recently returned from being Ma Kiddar and had some of the glories of a beery discussion still about her, she felt, but she fumbled and talked thick, and the kids were frightened watching her. Worse, she was still out. The girls were ready for bed and she wasn't there. When she came in, annoyingly for her only a couple of minutes late, and he made chill comment, very likely she was inwardly supported not merely by the Demon Alcohol, but by a lot of anti-husband talk from the Ma gang in the back-end bar. So off we went. Cold criticism, swift answer, each side scoring points and making hurts according to the methods peculiar to each sex. As a debate it was entirely useless, for what outcome can there be in a conflict between opponents possessing the opposite polarity of a different sex? Either the line is live and produces the physical spark of a blow or a kiss, or it goes negative in a mutual departure. These two could not depart: such a motion was not in their tradition. In front of the kids they could not kiss. Well, then—one night I came home to find the usual scene being enacted. I was a little late, though; in that red-papered angry room the tension between the seated, tight-lipped man and the flushed, brazen woman on her feet, but still not going, was at the point of violence. As I took my seat, the flash came. There was a mighty uprising of male, a late quailing of woman, the kids' crescendo, and something new this time. I found myself on my feet and using all the weight I had to thrust the angry man out of his path.

The attack had some success because it was unexpected and he was off-balance. In his surprise he turned and half-raised his fist so that it struck my jaw. I think that half-blow appalled him. He stood back, and I, though thinking miserably that my jaw must be dislocated, took a little more of the ring. I was white, I felt white. In that moment, the little girls fell silent, their mother slipped round the door and was gone.

My father turned, said something to the effect that I had no call to put my oar in, and reached for his pipe. The girls shuffled off their sofa to make for bed—show over for that night. I sat down to undo my bootlaces, and if anything more was said I cannot recall what it was, but only that I was overcome by the sensation of having made my debut on the stage of full manhood, pitchforked on you might say without benefit of rehearsal. I was nearly fourteen, and one part of my childhood ended that night.

Chapter Twelve

I LOOK ON FREEDOM FROM THE
END OF A PLANK

A journey can be so long that the man making it is made by it, so to speak, becoming adapted to the conditions of movement and upset when at last it ceases. Travellers-in-space, especially before speed was applied to their careers, often experienced that. The three-year-long cruise under sail, which the seaman thought he wished over, ended for him in a few days off-balance on terra firma, and was renewed right away in a fresh signing-on, perhaps for life. Travel too many leagues and there was always the likelihood of becoming a minor Wandering Jew, so fidgety-footed that the only destination to fit must be one that had the opposite qualities of motion and rest combined, a sort of geographical treadmill. Some of this sort still survive. No doubt they whirl the globe on wings and a snort, now, like minor satellites or Saturn's rings. But what are more common and come into everyone's regular encountering are travellers-in-time who have a similar knack of signing-on for another date whenever the calendar catches up with their first intention. There's the chap who won't spend this week's overtime money until such time as he can do so without leaving himself near-broke, in ten years, say, in twenty, no, in thirty; the loving couple who are going to have a family when they get a house, when they have it properly furnished, when the car is paid for, the television set; the fellow who is going to give his wife a real holiday when the children are grown up, when he's retired, when his rheumatism is better; or old moaner who is going to ask for his cards when—when it suits him, that's when. The arrival at a time-destination is not what it promised to be. Very likely the traveller cannot remember what that promise was, or why it struck a light for him at such a remote distance. But he is very well aware that the familiar unwinding of days, weeks, months and years has stopped: he looks out on the great stillness of Now. It isn't nice, you know. Hope deferred maketh the heart sick; hope fulfilled leaveth the belly vacant.

So it was with me when my clock threatened to strike fourteen. I was one of a company of time-travellers who had wended our way over several ages, that is, if you allow that the hours of childhood ripen as slowly as plums upon a wall and the sun often stands for hours in the sky when children play. All this extenuated great while, we looked forward to leaving school. That was the glimmer at the end of the tunnel, so faint that there were periods when one didn't even bother to imagine reaching it. Now with the passing of the thirteenth birthday, it seemed to be suddenly rushing upon us. Every week almost, one or other of the slightly-older lads disappeared over Time's weir. Some strict contemporaries, too, because of a rule that orphans and half-orphans might leave school at thirteen. It would come to all of us anon, no doubt of it. That was disturbing.

The first of the Battle-axe members to go was Harry Allen. True, he stayed around with us as long as he could. He got a job in a glass-and-china emporium and at once set about helping himself to some of the goods (including the Battle-axe regalia aforementioned). His motive for thieving was not profit, in fact, I think he wanted principally to impress us with the privileges and opportunities that belong to the worker. He was caught, convicted, and sent to a training-ship, from whence he emerged two years later ruined by worse vices than his own, a shocking little sailor-pansy.

Charley Dodd left next, for a job in a small engineering factory. What he knocked off was of no interest to anybody, and no value, except that it showed he had the run of the place and really *did* work. Nearly all the lads during the first year of their employment kept something in their pockets that indicated its nature. That was all he was after. He spent quite a lot of time in our company still, but was obviously growing away from us towards gambling sessions and girls. He had his long trousers, you see. With us, you got breeched out of the first week's pay you earned; that was the sign of your economic and sexual maturity. If you didn't wear long trousers, the girls wouldn't look at you, not even if they were less than your age.

They, too, were undergoing a similar disturbance to the one that fluttered us, though with them the biological side of it was more important than the economic. They still played games in the street, but they began to look wrong for there. At thirteen, some of them were mature enough, some rather miserably so, because it might happen that they still had to wear the childish frocks and pinafores which put an obscene touch to their budding bosoms and swelling calves. 'Tch! Tch!' the matrons tutted together as they watched Lily or Edna wrestling with a small boy, and the flush and fullness of their cheeks, the newly-cumbered sway of their bodies adver-

125

tised the disgusting presence of womanhood in the short, torn frocks. There was a certain amount of experiment with these bright lassies, which had its dangers for them, but most got safely into the next bracket, fourteen and working. At that, in a leap, they were years ahead of us. They walked in pairs along the lovers' lanes to be whistled at and pursued by lads of fourteen, fifteen, sixteen. The fourteens had almost no chance. For them, there would be a miserable year of perpetual rebuff which drove most of them into bashfulness and salutary inhibition for the time being.

It was this cycle that Charley was being drawn into. We saw less and less of him in the evenings. At school, of course, nothing. There I had been left to sustain the reputation we made as a team on my own. This was easy enough as it turned out. My state of permanent rebellion against the discipline and dullness of lessons was partly mitigated, once the scholarship question was over and done with, by a willingness on the part of the teachers to accept me more or less on my own terms. It seemed now to be generally known that I would work only at subjects that interested me. This didn't strain me any. Subjects I was interested in numbered one: English composition. If proficiency in that was a passport to the teacher's esteem, it had the other advantage of being no interference in my relationship with fellow-pupils. They considered I couldn't help it, any more than Willie White could help drawing well. But the real reason why writing became such a passport lay in the character of the headmaster, in these latter years increasingly a power in our affairs.

Mr. Gillespie was popular with the boys, certainly, being the sort of man in authority who could squat down to a game of marbles with any of us and lose nothing of his natural majesty afterwards. He was pleasant and easy moving among us but in his anger he could be a pretty terrible figure. Experts testified that he could put more sting into a lashing than any other teacher in the town. You see, his wrath was that of the just man outraged. What moved him to corporal punishment was almost always behaviour of the kind he called 'shabby'. You could steal apples from Jameson's orchard—he'd give you a lecture consisting largely of hints on how not to be caught. But if you allowed the blame to be put on other boys by lying or by default of owning-up, you were for it—that was 'shabby'.

The noble fellow had an equal passion for good verse and for poor puns. At any time, the top class was liable to be held up by the appearance of his tall, eager figure in the doorway, a copy of *Punch* in his hand or Wordsworth on his tongue. Say, it was a dark, snivelling sort of morning—he'd read us out a couple of *Punch* jokes to cheer us up. I don't remember that anyone actually laughed at these things, but we were all willing to, all saw how right it was of him to be amused, and we did feel cheered up. Or, perhaps, it was a fine, restless day, the marvellous new stare of April in our window-panes and even the class-room air shuddering a little to breezes miles away—the door shot open. 'Oh, to be in England', he'd begin, like the Prologue in the opera, and go on to quote Browning, Wordsworth, Shelley, whoever came to mind and was any-ways apposite. Even the dumbest were impressed by the true enjoyment he had in these otherwise fat-headed strings of words. He was a real teacher, we felt, couldn't help being one; the others just did it for money and out of a dislike of boys.

His interest in the written word made him welcome the slightest show of skill in producing it. Sometimes when I had turned in a rather better effort than average, he would hold the whole school in the hall while he read it to them. I think some of the teachers expected me to develop a swollen head over these performances. No doubt I had the pleasant sensation of feeling some of my parsnips being buttered, but the thing was so eccentric to the ordinary course of school events, and so obviously led nowhere, my pride in it was chiefly the small one of having pleased one of us queer characters for whom words were more than words. It was between him and me and the gate-post—the gate-post being that far-distant and miraculous folk who actually wrote books.

This inclusion into the headmaster's select but potty group of people who found something fine in the flow of a phrase was one of several signs by which I was becoming uncomfort-ably aware that there were attractions upon me that pulled in unknown directions and threatened to take me out of the orbit my fellow corner-lads so naturally swung into. My enthusiasms were beginning to strike them as too intense. The stories we all read were too real for me, I was made to feel when my mates began to develop an adult scorn if I went on too long about something I'd been reading. In the same way, the last of the secret codes I devised for our clan (it con-sisted of letters drawn from the authentic Babylonian cuneiform) was too elaborate. The clansmen admired, but without the true enthusiasm or the intention to make it their own. I think it was becoming apparent to them that I had a life of my own that they wouldn't want to share, particularly not now when they were near entering upon an early man-hood that they most decidedly wanted to be orthodox.

I certainly had my own secret life which I never talked of. For instance, though most of us owned some sets of lead soldiers, theirs were long ago smashed up in vigorous cannon-ades and rough handling; mine were almost intact, preserved by my need that they should play many parts and always live again for tomorrow's battles. Besides I played for preference by myself so that I could keep up a stream of commentary necessary for me if I was to get the game up to the requisite imaginative intensity. What's more, I didn't even need these little models. Often I collected some dozen boxes of matches of various kinds that came with the groceries and with them for armies could re-enact the rise and fall of the Roman Empire, the Norman Conquest, Clive in India, or invented-battles of my own. Square safety matches could represent disciplined troops such as the Romans; round, fair-headed Puck matches were Vikings or Goths; the smaller varieties of each, Egyptians or Indians. I've sat in my bedroom so fascinated with these combinations and the old tales they were re-living for me, that daylight had ebbed away for everyone else and my long quiet had persuaded the household I must be out. When I did break off and appeared in the next room blinking in the gaslight, my eyes drugged with in-seeing, I must have looked like Wells's time-traveller returned from riding the impossible abysses of lost ages.

Another habit that grew on me without anyone noticing it, was a trick of sliding off on my own most Saturday nights. Saturday probably because Charley went shopping with his mother that night and the general communal stir of a city on the spend pulled at me if I stayed on the corner-end or 'minded the hoose' with a pal. It was better to be by oneself, to travel long empty streets into the crowds and out again, because so doing you got a more vivid sense of your own being and even the foresight of what your becoming might be. The younger you are the more important it is that you should consort with your unrealized selves. Friends prevent that by their presence. They can't help insisting that you play the part they know as you and which is all the miserly economy of communication has so far allowed you to publish to them. But you are nipped in the rear by potentials you cannot get at when in company. Why, a boy's soul is as rich with possible men-to-come as a hen's gut with eggs; in loneliness he can let some of them rehearse an imaginary life, and must do if his future is to be a full one.

That's what I was up to many a windy night going down Jesmond Vale under the maw of rushing blacknesses and the flutter of gas-flames imprisoned like fire-moths in glass cases; or turning the corner where a bland moon stood over the tiles of the Blue Bell at the top of Shields Road, the trams tottered down among the shopping crowds and newsboys flew like embodied shrieks crying 'Futbarl-ee-ay!'; or in and out the impeded traffic of Grainger Street, that same moon standing now over the black tower of St. John's, looking on tumult. Often I made my journey more amusing by a small boy's trick. I'd pick out someone to follow, and endeavour to stay on his trail unobserved by him. It might be a pal of mine accompanied by his mother, more usually an interesting stranger. The game was to creep along behind the quarry, taking cover whenever he looked round, anticipating the next move and sometimes boldly coming abreast. There were hazards, of course: I might be hiding in a shop doorway when an assistant told me to scoot; or if my cover was an engaged couple going arm in arm, and I was stepping in behind them, they might become aware that someone was pacing their paces. They broke and swung round, showing me up plain. There was usually a stage, too, when the quarry became uneasy, feeling himself followed. I've known a chap get seriously worried at this unremitting and to him invisible pursuit. If it was a woman I followed, she arrived at that stage earlier, but was also quicker to spot who was after her, and then I had to give up at once before she told a copper.

This was a game for the crowded streets. I practised it most often on the Shields Road–Byker Bridge approach to town. There were other routes open to anyone with a pair of feet and time to spare. Each had its advantages, Newcastle being a fine town to roam in, especially after dark. Its natural features are excellent, that's why, since it is all hills, vales, bridges and one view succeeds another every hundred paces in a manner which fascinates anyone with an eye for composition in a landscape. True, for two centuries or more the main endeavour of the city fathers has been to destroy this balance, and the muck of unrefined capitalism of all periods is pretty thick on all quarters. Still, there is a natural obduracy in the configuration of the place which resists all the erosions and excrescences which otherwise must have made a Hull or a Birmingham of it. Often I went a bit out of my way in order to give some quality of exploration to the trip. I might make for the heights of St. Peters first, up the sordid and happy Headlam Street where they took my mother the day they ran her in. From St. Peters you looked down a hillside of staggered roofs and cobbled streets to where the river slid like new-boiled pitch under ships and quays until it took the glitter of the lights on several bridges, high and low, or writhed with reflected flame as a train passed over. That was the basic scene, but as you descended, its angles and emphasis shifted. Bridges moved their relation to one another; quays and the shipping flattened out, losing the river behind them; and the centre of the town began to rise up. Then on the river-side itself, when you were near enough to smell its dankness and the touch of salt that blew up from it and to see its scum of corks and contraceptives and half-wrecked crates washing under the sterns of foreign ships, the bridges were now high overhead. You saw, too, that it was a fortress-city you were making for. There was a climb ahead of you before you got into the inner gaiety of crowds. Either you toiled up Dean Street, which was a sort of glacier of asphalt and cobble-stones coming down steeply and ponderously by a cliff of office buildings and through a black railway arch before it could spread itself out on an easier gradient; or you could try your wind and leg-muscles on the Dog Leap Stairs, in which latter case you emerged just where the old keep of the original 'new' castle sits in its breast-high mesh of shining railway-lines.

That was probably the oldest path to town. Other nights I took the newest, through the clean air of the parks and crossing the Ouseburn by Armstrong Bridge, that is over the tops of cherry-trees and a cackling of geese at a farmhouse below. Or to avoid people altogether, I dipped down into the darkness of the Vale, over a bridge so small and low it bent to the muttering intimacy of little waters.

Of course, all these routes ran westward and into the jostle of Saturday night. It was a working-class crowd in every street, largely cheerful because, being Saturday, they had a bob or two to chuck away; and easy with one another because they had all got that bob or two the same hard way, or similar, were none of them any better than they should be, because they all spoke the same dialect, and because this was 'canny Newcassel'. Not Scotland, by the way, and 'canny' has not here the miserable meaning to which the Scots have debased it, but is the true English opposite of 'uncanny'. Anybody that is canny is all right, believe me, and sufficient of this crowd were to make it pleasant to be with.

Whatever point I joined them, terrier-fashion at heels and kerb or squeezing by, I let myself be carried along on their tide until it whirlpooled within the naphtha-lit stalls of the Bigg Market. A fascinating assembly of highly-coloured hucksters then filled the acre of cobbles in front of the Town Hall. The press of people coming into it became instantly ruddy-faced and bright-eyed as the naphtha-flares fanned out, eating the air just overhead, their smoke visibly coiling up to a brazen sky. Yet the confusion of light and smoke was almost outdone by the competitive racket of cries and spiels going up from all those stalls. The beauty of it was that all this vocalized salesmanship was concerned with giving stuff away.

130

A fellow with leather lungs and a straw hat ceaselessly com-
piled huge bags of confectionary, which he proceeded to give
away (except that as a matter of form he took a shilling back
each time) right and left and three rows back of the crowd.
Next to him a herbalist, hoarse as a crow, logically recom-
mended his cough candy as invaluable and practically costless.
Rival ice-cream wagons, their gilt and cream and blue almost
a coloratura cry on the lit air, echoed to Italian-tinted Tyne-
side as their crews of brisk dark men flung bigger and bigger
dollops into brass sandwich-makers and unhesitatingly let the
public know exactly what was being given away to them.
There were whelk-stalls, scent-stalls, fruit-stalls, drink-stalls,
clothing-stalls, all advertising vocally this fever of Saturday
philanthropy they all shared. And one among them all was
mute—the second-hand book-stall.

Sooner or later, I always got round to there. Indeed, lighter
traffic tended to get squeezed out that way. Its patrons, you
see, were quiet shoveable people, and it stood next to the
biggest whelk-stall, at the back of which was a backwater of
relative darkness which some folks found handy at times. In
its twilight you might see a dark figure in a shawl sucking up
mussels with modesty, or a little boy being fumbled with so
that he could have a pee, or a bowler-hatted bloke gushing
like a water-closet, as he shot out a mixture of pork pie and
beer and clutched the back of his neck after each vomit. If
you didn't care for these sights you turned to the books. This
was legitimate in my case, though boys' attention was properly
to be discouraged, because I did now and then buy. I think
the proprietor had even some sympathy with me, he so
patiently watched my progress from the three-and-sixpenny
rows, where it was unthinkable I'd make a purchase, all the
way down to the tuppenny and penny boxes, and was so
pleased to see me pick up anything worthy of the name 'book'.
In this way, and perhaps to please him, I once bought Carlyle's
Sartor Resartus. I didn't read it, then or ever, but Carlyle
still has a strong smell of mussels for me.

After the Bigg Market, I hurried through the series of
covered markets before they closed. If I hadn't spent my
coppers already, there was a couple of kiosks in the Flower
Market where they sold old copies of *Dick Turpin, Claude
Duval*, etc., for a ha'penny each. They also sold filthy
literature of excellent quality: *De Maupassant, De Kock,
Gautier*, and, of course, the pornographer's Bible, *Aristotle's
Works*. They were a bit dearer, though, and not yet the para-
mount necessity they became in another year or so.

The Green Market, over the way, was worth a call because
Uncle George had a pitch there. If a nephew hung around till

131

he wasn't busy, he might easily collect some free fruit. After which he slid—to the Bird Market. An incredible joint, that. It stood on a corner above the Fish Market, which by the time I got there would be dead except for cleaners swilling water around behind its iron grilles. But upstairs, the Bird Market windows were fairly at bursting-point with a fullness of smoky light. A narrow staircase led up to this place, and so many people were coming and going upon it, you would find yourself halted on one foot before the other could get a toe-hold between several sets of heels. What lived at the top of them was a sort of sweet-noted pandemonium. The walls were hung with tiers of cages, most of them tiny, which contained a various flutter connected with canaries, linnets, and the finches, bull, gold or green, all singing madly so as to get themselves sold quick. From tier to tier layers of smoke thick as felt, stretched and sagged or floated. Under and in that smoke were the bird-fanciers, most of them pitmen, as you could see whenever they removed their caps to scratch their heads and the blue coal scars showed up. They all smoked, they all spat, they all swore. And they did these things faster when a knot of them gathered together in wonder before a bird that really was a mazer. How they could hear that particular warbler out of all the rest was a mazer to me, but it seemed they could, these connoisseurs of the canary-voice, or, at least, they let on they could, and you can't contradict a pitman.

There were no women present, in fact, it was doubtful if a woman could have lived in that atmosphere, not for long, anyway. But at times, a couple would appear in the doorway, searching. If you were next to them, you'd hear one say, 'Can ye see him, Bella?' And presently, 'There he is—A thowt he'd be amang the bords', followed by the hail, 'Hey, Geordie, howway man, ye'll miss the train.' Geordie, whichever one of that large ilk he was, took not the slightest notice. The intruders moved off muttering.

My last call was again at the Bigg Market to see what I could pick up. The stalls were being dismantled now; many small fry used to collect in the hope of treasure trove, a fancy box, some bruised fruit, or something of real value that had been overlooked among the straw, paper and broken boxes. After that came the two-mile walk home, by Byker Bridge this time, periodically pursued and left behind by the melancholy trundling of trams. If I'd bought or scrounged anything eatable I munched as I walked; if I'd bought books they were tucked up my jersey; and generally by this time I tried to discount tiredness by the old method of skipping the cracks in the pavement and counting how many steps or hops it took me to get from one tram-standard to the next.

At the corner of our street, where the blue glare of the Junction first became visible, I was often joined by our cat, a ginger animal of great strength and sagacity. He got these qualities out of the training we gave him when he, and we, were younger. We used to tie him to a box containing a couple of flat-irons, and nip his nail till he moved off with the load. That so developed his muscles he became king cat of Third, master of a considerable harem and mighty proud. But he didn't forget the founder of his fortune; he'd always leave his beat in order to escort me as far as the door before departing again into a garden in response to a low, seductive mew. So there I was at my own door—what lay behind it?

That was always the question in my mind. More often than not, I'd already horrified myself with imagined disasters en route. In that case, very likely there'd be a comfortable anticlimax: the evening would end with my mother and I sitting by the fireside as of yore, taking our supper off a chair and both reading. Her book never held her attention for long. She'd have a talk of her own past, of her abiding wonder at the cruelty of the world, its streaks of astonishing kindness, the general non-understandability of folk, or—this increasingly as I grew to man's estate—of my future. She was anxious that I, who had once justified her by obstinately remaining alive and growing up to solid good health against what she feared was the run of the play, should now somehow excuse her short-comings and take some of the blame off her by making a success of my life. God is good, that she held to, the Lord knows why. She hadn't understood why He had tortured her for so many years, but there must be an inscrutable purpose in it and a Blessing to emerge somewhere. Not that she had any hope the Blessing would be for her, but for, perhaps, her son?

So far there hadn't been a sign of it, I mean not that any reasonably clear-headed person, such as my father to take the nearest outstanding example, could see. I was a corner-lad, not more than one step off trouble, unapproved of by the neighbours and in no credit at school. Add to that, my possession of a queer streak which would probably bring me to still more no good and you'd got the complete view of me as held by the impartial and fair-minded observer. Against that, all a woman could urge was her secret and somewhat theological faith that there was justice in the universe ultimately and it ought to be on my side. She sat by the fire poking the dead ashes away and she could see it, she could see the brightness coming, surely, but not how or where. 'That's all granny,' said my father, who looked at the clock, not on the hot crumbling of coals, and knew that the travelling minute brings the hour up, when it strikes, what you've done, you've done, no reward to the idler.

Now this last of my school-years saw a curious strengthening of my mother's case, if you could call it a case. In fact, the household was being threatened with one of those exasperating instances of the woman being always right which bring most families to fury on occasion. My sisters brought home stories of my somewhat eccentric successes at school. One of these brought me a money prize, small, but you can't ignore cash. My father, now taking real notice, doubled it out of his own pocket; then took charge of both amounts, they being in the form of War Savings Certificates, and reserved them for my future. So to that extent he was on mother's horse now. Then after my last exam there arrived such an astonishingly good report, it left both parents flapping.

How pleasant it would be if I could claim that I achieved that last triumph out of a determination to give them pleasure. But such a virtuous notion, which I at once took credit for, mind you, was far from my mind. The facts were plainer and more in accord with human nature round our part of the world. This was what happened. The top class of the school competed among themselves for a captain's medal, and the winner stayed on for another six months if he happened to be of leaving age at the time of the examination. There was some individual rivalry (which I didn't share), and also the old battle between the groups. Not that they cared a hoot about scholarly achievement of any sort, but they took on each other at any contest which was going; and for this one, in which few had any chance of winning, they nominated a champion. Our gang chose me. It was a nuisance because it meant that I had to do some work so as to make a show. They, of course, devised a lot of plans for helping me by crooked means, but these were not to be relied on because the teacher taking that exam was an ex-pupil and graduate of the corners who knew his lads well and not by hearsay. Well, unwillingly I got down to the job with no hope of pipping the favourite, but bound, by oath to the Battle-axe, to get into the running if I could.

Never having tried work on this all-round scale before, the effect astonished me nearly as much as it did the teachers. Half-way through I was an even chance, neck-and-neck with the favourite, and no sign of either of us missing a fence. As each day's papers were returned to us marked up, our totals continued to be dead level. We were out ahead of the field, just the two of us. But on the final session we both slipped a bit and each thought he'd thrown the race away. I was right

134

as it happened. My name stood a good second on the list, and the gang were happy enough to see that. It was fair, anyway: my flash-in-the-pan effort on the last few weeks at school should not have beaten a lad who'd always worked steady. He got his just reward and I could relax for the next ten years or so.

The trouble was that I couldn't. Our little world of the street was seething with inner turmoil because of the pull there was on so many of us to put away childish things and go to be little men together in the greater world of Work. Anyone who still had some toys left raffled them off. Certain celebrated collections of *Magnets* and *Gems*, of cigarette cards, marbles, were hurriedly disbanded. Even catapults and airguns came under this new scorn. Bold lads felt their chins and complained of the condition of the old man's razor, or cursed the copiousness of their emissions. There was a lot of 'training' going on, too. Lads had no shame in being seen plodding around on solitary runs in plimsolls, or announcing that they did physical jerks every morning, or took a cold bath some evenings. The bathers down by the Ouseburn counted their pubic hairs in public to compare crops. On the corners there was a continual series of 'dares' running on, not the old follow-my-leader kind of thing, but a measuring up of individual in man-to-man competition. And one and all seemed to have picked a job for themselves: they knew what they were going to be.

Except me. I emerged from my bout of late-blooming scholarship into the summer holidays, having scorned an invitation to stay on at school for another six months, with only the vaguest of notions that presently I'd get a job. Yes, but at what? The survivor of nine years' educational slavery found the simple choice of which freedom to take just impossible to make. My recent fame had spread round the family so visiting relatives naturally wanted to know what now. Surely I must have an ambition. Surely, I must, I thought. What about the footplate? As an engine-driver's son I had a hereditary right to that job, if fit and well. I was fit and well, all right, but I couldn't see myself working on the same railway as my father. Nor in a job with anybody else's father, come to that. 'What's thoo ganna be, Bill?' asked my Sunderland Uncle Will, and for him I had a brilliant inspiration. 'An armature-winder,' I said, not knowing what on earth that was. He nodded; it satisfied him, and I had space to breathe again.

One night my rare Uncle Robin turned up. Rare? Oh, yes, certainly: read on. As he hadn't been around for a couple of years or so, my mother re-introduced me with a build-up I

135

didn't welcome. She trotted out a prize essay of mine for him to read and said in a boasting way that surprised me, 'And he's an atheist, too; doesn't believe in the Bible.' Well, that from her! The school-stuff was a poor enough gambit since it could only lead to awkward askings about what work I proposed taking up; now there'd be another belly-aching interrogation to probe my beliefs, part one, lack of. You see, I'd forgotten the peculiar quality of my Uncle Robin. He was an atheist. He was a socialist; he was a vegetarian; he was a physical culturist; he was—in short, he was a crank. 'A crank,' quoted he, not long after this, 'is a little thing, but it makes revolutions.'

He invited me round to his place and I found it bore him out to the extent of being not unlike a revolutionist's workshop. Not that there were bombs about, or anything sinister, no. In the nature of things a working-class revolutionary cannot command the means of effective violence, and well he knows that. If he ever applies violence at all, it is tardily in his own defence. What was evidenced here in the small particulars, was a kind of life obstinately different from the working-class households all around. Uncle Robin was a working-man all right, an electrician by trade, and a very good one. He was never out of work, and he earned good money—as they called it. But there was no woman in his house. He was a bachelor by persuasion, you might say, convinced by observation that marriage and the barrow-load of kids you used to get with it was so often a sort of intellectual suicide for the working-man of that period. It isn't comfortable being a bachelor unless you're very well-heeled or the girls you get around among have good jobs themselves. To live in digs is almost as bad as being married without the fun: it entails a similar adjusting of your habits to those prevailing in the neighbourhood. Therefore, you found my Uncle Robin established in lonely state generally as tenant of a couple of rooms above a shop, which advantageous location allowed him to make as much row as he liked over week-ends.

He had no end of hobbies; he was always working at them any old time of day or night; he played the piano, the violin, the phono-fiddle; and he was liable to encourage these practices in the many friends, little nephews and nieces and their friends, who so frequently called on him. All this activity was unnatural, the neighbours thought, that's why he liked the nearest neighbour to be an empty shop. Of course, he had other periods when a relative solitude set in. Friends married; children grew up and took to other whims. Robin still sat at his own hearth reading queer philosophies, or perhaps on a Sunday he'd pin up sheets of music all round the walls and spend hours going round this gallery with his fiddle, having a concert all to himself. He was a musician by right. The old Northumbrian tradition is that the youngest son of the family, the one least needed for work or for war, should be the minstrel. In obedience to it, when Robin was old enough my grandfather made him a fiddle and set of Northumbrian pipes, never being in the least bothered by the fact that musical instrument making was not his trade. That fit the lad up for playing at a curran supper or amusing the ingle-neuk of a winter's night.

Because he was the youngest of the family, the poke-shakings as they say, Robin had not the large physique of his brothers and sisters. As I saw him at that time, he was a thin man in slippers, clothes rather loose on him, sparse brown hair wisping over baldness, a gingery moustache under a somewhat equine nose, and his expression often rather more intent than his purpose because one eye turned in, making the other take all the note that was to be taken. Not a handsome man, but extremely kindly, with such a depth of good humour in him that even in the cut-and-thrust of the most savage argument he could always turn the stab away by an easy cheerful saying. He was forever making little gifts to people, too, and must have been a regular mine of pennies to all the kids that had the luck to know him. Within the limits of his crankihood he was hospitable. I've no doubt that when I first went to see him in my new character of a nearly-adult atheist, he set me down to a meal of some sort or other.

But what sort? That for the orthodox was a question. As a vegetarian and bachelor, he did his own cooking. As a disciple of Thoreau, he did as little as possible. As a disciple of several hundred food-reform leaders, he knew that life is well sustained on fewer meals than is customary, and that ninety per cent of ordinary eating is of harmful substances such as sugar, salt, meat, white flour, et (considerably) cetera. Being a host as well, he had to make some compromise. That made, so that you got sugar (deleterious) in your (poisonous) tea for instance, his table still held a number of matters that were strange and revolutionary then. Shredded Wheat, Post Toasties, Grape Nuts, and other of the breakfast cereals which nobody ate until housewives discovered how much easier they were to handle than porridge; Marmite, then a Bovril-drinker's nightmare, and on no account to be mixed up with the soup or spread on bread as he did; and Mapleton's fruit and nut cakes, compressed concoctions so liable to rouse a contemporary suspicion that they hadn't even been cooked. I was by no means put off by these strange foods. Nor was I by my uncle's famous tea-cup which was quite black inside

137

with a tannin-deposit of years that wouldn't come off in any ordinary wash-up and gave its owner an excellent illustration of the bad effect tea has on the stomach when he wanted to make that point to his guests. Having established that truth, he supped noisily from the cup, crouching over it as though he feared to spill a drop. Like all wise men he enjoyed his own inconsistencies.

There were rows and rows of books about us where we sat, books and magazines. The number of them was astonishing for a working-class room and their contents were more surprising still. You'd perhaps expect Jack London and Wells, Blatchford and William Morris, the Rubaiyat and Whitman, Thoreau, Shelley, Kropotkin, Winwood Reade, Haeckel, Belfort Bax, any amount of socialist pamphlets and Rationalist Press publications, some of these stalwarts certainly. But all around and overlaying them was a weird assemblage of works on theosophy, transcendentalism, anthroposophy, spiritualism, Yoga, Flat-earthism, physical culture, the revelations about the deadly effect of salt, sugar, meat, feather-beds, starch, and the alternative advocacy of raw food, grass or yeast. One or other of these was always being taken down to illustrate a point in my uncle's argument, and given to me to take home. A pile of them accumulated by my chair. Whether I wanted to read so variously or not, I had to be loyal enough to make a shot at them, and some, of course, I was eager for and really needed.

You are not to suppose that Robin believed all this stuff. Far from it. He delighted in a new approach to old problems, no matter how unlikely its premises, was able to suspend his disbelief until he'd mastered the thought in it and then he took pleasure in demonstrating the flaws. I wasn't equal to debating these odd philosophies with him, but that didn't matter. He was a good talker and I liked listening. His special quality was a gift for exposition which I've never known surpassed, not even by people who have won a lot of fame for their performances in this line. His frequent loneliness no doubt gave him the opportunity to formulate his thought; the fact that he was a technician as well as a philosopher kept it unusually clear. Anyway, I've known him plunge into an account of something really difficult, the Theory of Relativity for instance, and make such a show of it that I came away into the black slum streets outside convinced that I understood it all, did understand it in fact, until the necessity we have of re-formulating in my own words made it woolly again. The crystal fogged, melted to my hot fumbling, and melted Einstein is nothing to see the heavens through.

All the same, I was having some very wide horizons opened

to me. I enjoyed this increased power of mental vision, but—it lifted no veil on my future. Worse than that, it deepened my introspection. It took me farther away from my own generation. Was I another eccentric like Uncle Robin? According to mother there had always been a queer streak in the Kiddars; according to Granny there was never any accounting for them—perhaps Robin and I were exceptionally twisted twigs on a family tree. It was our luck to have inherited an extra share of whatever genes were peculiar to the breed. Well, obviously, one way of finding out what I might become was to find out first what I was. Or to put it in a more approachable term, what is a Kiddar?

Many a sunny afternoon I wasted, ploughing through books in the public library for the slightest reference to the clan. Kiddar is a Northumbrian name; not many have borne it at any time: so wherever it was recorded, I could be reasonably certain that my family was meant. Here and there for two centuries back I stumbled on their traces. Well, and how was their luck? They'd impressed their contemporaries, by feats of strength, by their longevity, by the readiness of invention they showed in agricultural pursuits. Yes, but had they any money? No, not left over. Did they pay the rent? Not often. Had the world heard of them? No, they were just local. Beyond the two-century mark the records ran out, not of Kiddars, but because we were now in the period of the Border raids when the Scots burnt down churches and church registers. I was hot on the trail by this time, afire to find out more. Skip a century and there comes into the picture a family calling themselves Kydar—suppose they couldn't spell, as nobody could about then, were they not the same? To clinch it, some reference books said they were believed to be. If that was so, now, I could really take to myself some genuine, if rather far-fetched, tokens of fortune. For the Kydars (posh spelling) had titles, and castles, they had coats-of-arms. A coat-of-arms is sure proof that a family must have held winning cards once, the mere flash and dazzle of it must be designed to tempt more court cards into the hand. But when did they give it up, my branch, I mean—I had got as far as thinking of my branch. I asked Uncle Robin if he remembered anything of the sort in his time. He thought. Yes, he remembered something; he remembered a great seal, used as a door-stop, which had a coat-of-arms on it.

There you are, I thought, and came home that night through the fish-and-chip-scented air of a hot August twilight, my head full of feudal splendours and a conviction that I was ancestrally correct to ask for a better turn-up of the dice than normally came to one of my condition. Then the humpty-dumpty of hubris had me. I told my tale to mother in a bit of supper-time garrulity, and she capped it effectively at once. 'Wey, your grandfather was the son of a lord, come to that. A don't think Johnson was his real name, some mystery about it. A don't know. Ma started to tell me once, but she wouldn't say any more. I meant to ask her again, but, eh, well, it's too late now. Wouldn't do us any good anyway, likely not.'

That was just too much. I might believe in remote feudal ancestors, or kid myself I did, but a real genuine, nineteenth-century lord in the family tree was more than my socialist blood could stand for. I went off to bed repudiating this idea all over. It was a gum-tree I'd been up, for it is really a very common thing for proletarian families to have traditions of a noble origin. They are true, too, in the way that all traditions are true, that is, they express the broad truth that every-one is related to everyone else if you go far enough back, and the narrower principle that whereas the well-to-do family need not go far back to find a progenitor worth pinning the name to, a proletarian outfit has to climb a whole lot of generations before they come across one of the ilk who was in Fortune's lucky way.

Well, then, I was pursuing a hopeless trail. History was not going to cast my horoscope for me yet that had to be done now my fourteenth birthday had come and gone.

Chapter Thirteen

WILLING EMPLOYER WANTED

By now all who had finished school that summer term along with me had jobs. I alone was left still holidaying in solitary fashion and postponing from day to day the decision which would cut the navel-cord attaching me to my childhood. Yet the motion of making that cut rehearsed itself within me continually. Vast ambitions moved upon my imagination as I read or walked; in some moods I felt that the world had lifted its horizons, anything was now possible to me. Anything? Yes, ultimately anything, but to begin in what way? I saw myself as an apprentice planter in Malaya; as a wireless telegraphist aboard ship; as the youngest astronomer in a Moroccan observatory; as librarian to an eccentric earl in Morayshire; as a mystery man of Fleet Street. Of course, these fancies collapsed as I fondled them. Later, staring at the vacant in my window-pane, I saw no glories to come, only the plain truth that I was a Kiddar; my heritage, the routine of the factory or some similar industrial hour-glass regularly turning the sands of uncelebrated and nearly-unconsequenced labour. Tomorrow I'd go and book my natural place at the very end of the rank and file. Clenched on this the hard crust that was my portion, I fell asleep. Yes, but tomorrow the swelling August morn dissolved away these night-nigglings; the confident air had a tropic in it, was spiced with the aroma of the remote seas it moved over; the tremendous prospects building up in its skies naturally got themselves reflected in the equally cloudy architecture of schemes shaping themselves upon my imagination. So another day of dreaming stayed decision.

Soon the school would open up again and I could no longer excuse myself with the story that I was having my holiday that I had a right to. Still, I couldn't budge. I began to avoid possible questioners by hastily crossing the street on their appearance. What are you going to be, Bill? When are you starting work? Just to hear these well-meaning inquiries had the effect of freezing my will within me. It took cramp. Even if I asked the question of myself that was enough to bring on this cold obstinate paralysis. What I needed, of course, was a kick from outside. Presently that kick came.

141

Earlier I mentioned our amiable family habit of reading in the water-closet. It was harmless in every respect except that it held up the traffic. In that case, the new claimant gave a yell down the yard, or three yells at intervals it could be before the bookworm with his breeches down was prevailed upon to disenthrone himself. The system worked all right provided all parties had a reasonable amount of time on hand. The awkward customer who hadn't, was my father. Because he had to be at work often in a matter of minutes, he held that the line should be kept clear for the express, so to speak. That was fair, and when we remembered we yielded the point.

However, one mid-day when he was washing and getting into his work-clothes and mother packed his bait-tin, I forgot this rule. Taking note of none of these warning activities, seeing no red light, I wandered out and disappeared amongst the washing which hung in the yard. Nobody spotted the move I suppose, because I was immediately hidden between blue-bag-scented sheets as I strolled along that billowing aisle and bent to dodge under the last prop what time the wet end of a blanket took a flap at my ear-hole. So I came unobserved to the place of meditations. The bare sun was too dazzling-bright for comfortable reading; I closed the door. I was soon lost in a story. The sunbeams shaped by the gaps in the door cut curious moted corridors aslant through the clear dusk in the closet and these chequered my page, no doubt assisting me into a half-hypnosis in which I forgot how long I'd been there.

There was a shout along the yard, a stagger of heavy steps in the washing-aisles—the express! I rose, half-blinded and one leg shooting pins and needles, my book fallen, both hands grabbing my trousers, but the door was being violently shaken. For the first time in front of children (but was I children?) my father let fly a string of real oaths. And followed them, as I struggled out with what was undoubtedly the logic of the occasion: 'It's high time you were out earning your living, instead of hanging about in the way of folks that have to keep you...' and more. But these words said it. I had no reply to make.

Nor any for my mother as I came through the kitchen, still buttoning my braces. She said gently, 'You knew he was on the 1.45 shift, and you know what he is—couldn't you have kept out of his way?' I picked up the morning paper in one unpremeditated snatch and went straight into my bedroom, sat down, spread out the paper at the Situations Vacant page, making these various motions with the certainty of a well-rehearsed actor who knows his cue. 'Situations Vacant—Boys', that was it. I knew the page very well these days, had studied

142

the curious descriptions advertisers put in of the various Strong Lads, Smart Boys and Office Youths they needed to complete their collection of what must be wax-work figures, surely, since I never met any of my own generation that could honestly or dishonestly, describe themselves in the terms set out here. So often I'd drifted off to the more colourful columns where men were asked for. Such men, horizontal millers, panel beaters, upper roughers, decomposing men, chamber-masters, bottom burnishers—oh, to be a bottom-burnisher and still young in the trade. Today, though, I went straight to the matter in hand. Here we were: five possibles duly ticked off. Read them again, forget three, write down the box numbers of the other two. Now, pen, ink and notepaper, and to number one I offer my future.

This is the letter I might have written:

44 Third Avenue,
Heaton,
Newcastle-on-Tyne,
20th August, 1917.

The Advertiser,
Box 1313,
North Mail.

Dear Sir,

With reference to your advertisement in today's *North Mail*, I beg to apply for the post. I am fourteen years of age, strong, healthy, bright, punctual, clean and willing. My parents are working-class, my environment is working-class, the school I have just left is working-class, and with your kind assistance I feel qualified to become working-class myself.

Because I have known poverty, I am certain to accept the small wage you intend to offer. Because I resent poverty, I am likely to join any organization or activity which has the object of making you pay bigger wages. Because I know how poverty cripples the humble, I intend to be ambitious, within limits, and ready to advance myself at your expense. As an un-convicted juvenile delinquent, I'd have no hesitation in using dishonesty to gain my ends, but as a mourner over convicted pals I know that the kinds of dishonesty open to the likes of us are so risky and over-policed as to be practically useless for the purpose of getting on in the world. Legal aggrandise-ment is suspect for a different reason. As a member from birth of the community of the streets I am aware that individual success for one of our sort, if contrived and not accidental, incurs a personal severance from the rest. That makes a man ridiculous, you know. The self-promoted working-man is as much a living anomaly as the wealthy priest, the socially-approved poet, the knighted scientist, or the bearded lady.

Hedged off, therefore, as I am from a conventional or an infamous success by these parallel electric fences, it is probable I shall tread the daily round for a regular pittance all my life —that suits you.

It is usual to enclose testimonials as to one's good behaviour and ability when asking for a job. I send my horoscope instead. What is important about a man is not how able he is, nor how hard-working, but what's his luck. Hard work gets a man a shovel, or a pick, or a pen, not a cheque-book, not often. As for ability, lives of failures either show talent snapped off at the stem by disease, accident and hard-upness, or diligence and competence skilfully patching up the faults of a poor heredity and never having enough years to make a job of it. The lives of great men, now, all show us how easy a matter greatness is. Monotonously it is the same story of the born idler at last persuaded to do a few weeks' work in which he discovers either that he has a natural endowment which makes the most difficult matters simple for him, or else that there is an idea in his head which his age, and none other, is waiting to welcome. For a lesser success the sun shines not so brightly, but in the same place.

That is why the god we all secretly acknowledge is Luck. Heredity and Environment are his archangels, but he can set even them aside when he will. Luck is the only god who visibly performs miracles every day. The poorest man in the kingdom, a fellow racked on his environment, cursed in his heredity, may be released from both by the magic of a string of figures: 2XX12XX21. Somehow his unconscious linked with the infinite, by no prayer, his pen pricked out this algebraic sesame and Luck tipped the whole pool his way. It happens. And that is Success, quite innocent and wholly blessed.

Rare, yes. Such a cornucopia of fortune doesn't come to all. But drips from it do. And whenever one does, it's a day undoubtedly. There are chaps whose only break in a long labouring life came with the magical flash past the post of an outsider. Some very reasonable careers have occurred only because the right girl turned up at the right moment. Even people who ignore Chance out of many bad experiences of it have known the times when darts drop in the doubles, the ball runs the right way, the foreman likes your face, or when the three-hundredth despairing kiss suddenly wins a wonderful response. Everyone has known these golden moments. They are undeserved and cannot be commanded.

Yet plenty of people do try to load the dice. You see, the fortunate man has children; he wants to make sure that his run of luck continues in them. Of course, if he's a dull bloke, he has by now come to the conclusion that it was his ability or his morality that did it. That man's a pest to his bairns. But if he's a little sharper than that, it's bound to occur to him that certain charms and amulets he sees around have something to do with it. He begins to decorate his offspring with some of the recognized tokens of luck, old school ties, refined manners and accents, scholastic degrees, the knowledge of some games and haunts, a membership of certain coteries. Each of these is intended to act as a lodestone to the lightning of luck. Collect a rosary of them and if they do not actually attract constant good fortune to their wearer, they'll certainly persuade all his competitors that they have. That's half the battle.

Well, now you already know that I wear none of these social amulets; and that the Archangels of Chance gave to me an unprofitable heredity and a stony environment. So far I cannot claim to have experienced any exceptionally toward event which might suggest that I'm a destined child of fortune. Nevertheless, as it is high time the luck of the Kiddars turned, that goes for all of them, I intend to live in every possible way as if it had; and to regard any unblessed existence such as most kinds of work still are, as worth only a temporary endurance.

It is this uncertain and qualified endurance I now place at your disposal. No doubt you'd prefer something better. Believe me, what I offer so frankly is what you are increasingly likely to get from any one of that host who might sign themselves as I do.

Yours truly,
Kiddar